THE
Shamer's
DAUGHTER

LENE
KAABERBOL

Typeset in Bembo by Avon DataSet Ltd,
Bidford-on-Avon, Warwickshire

Printed and bound in Great Britain by
Clays Ltd, St Ives plc

The paper and board used in this paperback by Hodder Children's
Books are natural recyclable products made from wood grown in
sustainable forests. The manufacturing processes conform to the
environmental regulations of the country of origin.

Hodder Children's Books
A division of Hodder Headline Limited
338 Euston Road
London NW1 3BH

A note from the author

Any teacher worth her salt knows that glaring at an unruly class is usually more efficient than shouting at them. One of my students once handed in an assignment ahead of time – a rare event, but I still managed to forget about it. When I collected the essays, there was of course no paper on her desk. I looked at her. She protested indignantly, and I realised my mistake. I tried to smooth things over, saying that I hadn't actually told her off. 'No,' she said. 'But you gave me The Look.' And she was right.

I think we learn the power of The Look when we are children, from the receiving end. My mother was a master at it. Exceedingly few of my childhood crimes went undetected – she could look right through me when she wanted to. And when she scolded me, she would always insist that I look her in the eye. 'Look at me!' she would snap, as if that was part of the punishment. 'Look at me when I'm talking to you!'

When Dina's mother, the Shamer of this tale, takes on a suspected criminal, her first words are usually: 'Look at me!' And pity the poor wretch when he does, because the power of her gaze is so potent that it can bring hardened murderers weeping to their knees. I have certainly used my writer's right to exaggerate and enhance, but I know for a fact that the Shamers have learned a trick or two from my mother. And although Shamer is not a registered profession, nor indeed a word you can find in the dictionary, still the power of The Look exists, in our world too.

I am no longer a teacher. I no longer glare at people for a living (though I sometimes do it for fun, or because I think they have it coming). These days, the writing pays the rent (and the cornflakes and the stewing steak, and various other odds and ends). I live in Copenhagen, in a beautiful old warehouse, just across the harbour from the royal residence. I can wave at the Danish queen while brushing my teeth (so far, she hasn't waved back). I've arranged my desk so that I can watch the ships and listen to the seagulls as I write. 'Why do you always write fantasy?' my friends sometimes ask. Because I like faraway places and faraway times. And because there is, at the heart of every fantastical lie, a core of real truth. Like the small shiver that goes through a child when an adult says: 'Look at me when I'm talking to you.'

ONE

The Shamer's Brat

Strictly speaking it wasn't really Cilla's fault that I was bitten by a dragon. It *was* probably sheer coincidence that she decided to throw a bucket of whey in my face on the very day the man from Dunark came. But every time my arm hurts . . . every time I miss Cherry Tree Cottage and the pear trees and the chickens we had . . . I get mad at Cilla all over again.

Cilla was the miller's daughter, the only girl in a brood of six. Maybe that was the reason why she had become such a pain. Every time Cilla wanted something, a slice of honey-bread, a silk ribbon, perhaps, or a new set of Prince-and-Dragon markers . . . well, all she had to do was flutter her eyelashes and make her voice all syrupy. Her eyes were periwinkle blue, and she had the most charming dimples when she smiled. Her dad was putty in her hands. And if anybody teased her or thwarted her in some way, she complained to a couple of her brothers. They had all worked in the mill practically from the time they could walk, and they thought nothing of tossing around sacks of grain as if they were filled with feathers. Nobody liked to cross them, not even my own brother Davin, who actually seemed to enjoy a good fight now and then. Most of the time, Cilla was in the habit of getting exactly what she wanted.

Normally, I gave her a very wide berth. But that day had been a bad day from the start. Mama had scolded me for leaving my shawl out by the woodshed the day before, so that it was now soaking wet. I got into a fight with Davin, and Melli, my four-year-old pest of a little sister, had picked the eyes off my old rag doll. So what if I was much too old to be playing with dolls – Nana was *my* doll, and Melli had taken her without even asking. I was so mad and so fed up with the whole family that I couldn't stay in the house with them. I stood for a while in the barn and shared my woes with Blaze, our brown mare, who had the sweetest of tempers and was very patient with most human beings. But then Davin led her out to graze among the pear trees in the orchard, and the barn became lonely and boring. I knew that if my mother caught sight of me, it would not take her long to find some task for me; she was of the opinion that work is the best cure for the sulks. Without really thinking about it, I set off down the road towards the village.

Birches is not a big town, but we do have a smithy, an inn and the mill, run by Cilla's parents, not to mention eleven different houses and farms of varying sizes. And then there are the places like Cherry Tree Cottage, some distance from the village yet somehow still a part of it. In almost all the houses were families, and almost all the families had children, some of them as many as eight or ten. You would think, with so many to choose from, that it would be possible for me to find a friend or two, or at least some playmates. But no. Not me. Not the Shamer's daughter. Two years ago I could still sometimes play with Sasia from the inn. But then it became more and more difficult for her to look me in the eyes, and after that things became kind of difficult. Now she avoided me completely, just like everyone else.

So, having walked about a mile through mud and gusty winds to reach the village, I had no idea what to do there. I rarely went there any more, except to run a few errands for Mama; and I ended up standing indecisively in the village square, trying to look as if I had merely stopped for a minute to catch my breath. Janos Tinker went by with his handcart, waving at me but not quite looking. At the smithy Rikert was shoeing the miller's grey gelding. He called my name and wished me a good afternoon, but stayed bent over his work the whole time. And then big fat drops of rain started to spatter the gravel, and I could no longer pretend to be basking in the sun. I headed for the inn, possibly just out of habit. The main room was nearly empty; a lone guest was having a meal, a big bear of a highlander, from up the Skayler range. Probably he had taken summer work as a caravan guard and was on his way home now. He cast a quick and curious glance my way, but even without knowing me, he instinctively looked away, avoiding my eyes.

Behind the counter, Sasia's mother was wiping glasses.

'Hello, Dina,' she said politely, her eyes strictly on the glass she was polishing. 'What can we do for you?'

What would she do if I said *Look at me*? But I didn't, of course. 'Is Sasia in?' I asked instead.

'No, I think she is over at the mill.' She jerked her chin in that general direction, still without looking at me.

I think that that is where things really started to go wrong. I could feel this harsh and bitter anger building inside, an anger fed by all those downcast eyes and backs so casually turned against me. I knew. I knew that it would be so much easier for them if I simply stayed away. But I hadn't asked for the damned Shamer's eyes; I couldn't help being my mother's daughter. I still remember vividly how I cried when Sasia would no longer play with me.

'What's wrong with me?' I had asked my mother.

'There is absolutely nothing wrong with you,' she said. 'You've inherited my gift, that's all.' She seemed both proud and sad. I wasn't proud, just lonely and miserable, and if I could have torn her so-called gift out of myself I would have done it, torn it out and cast it away, there and then and without hesitation. Unfortunately, that wasn't possible. I had my gift and I was stuck with it.

If I hadn't been so very angry, I might just have gone home. But a bitter sort of defiance was rising in me. So they would like for me to keep out of their way. So it would be so much easier for everyone. But what about me? Didn't I have a right to be here? Someone to talk to, someone to be with . . . it wasn't that much to ask, was it? So with my defiance burning like a hot lump in my throat I strode across the square and into Mill Street.

'Did you want something, Dina?' asked Ettie Miller when she saw me. She was busy getting the laundry off the line before the rain soaked it again.

'I'm looking for Sasia,' I said.

'I think they're all in the hay barn,' she answered indistinctly, her mouth full of clothes-pegs. And of course she kept her eyes firmly on her sheets and shirts and never once looked at me.

I crossed the yard and ducked in through the barn doors. The space inside was wrapped in gloom, but they had carved some turnip lanterns and stuck candles in them, making them look like glowing skulls. It looked cosy and scary all at once. On top of the hay cart Cilla sat enthroned, a pink sheet around her shoulders and a crown of ox-eye daisies on her gold-blonde hair. The rest of the girls were ranged in a semicircle around her, and in the middle stood Sasia, the miller's old felt hat on her head, trying to remember all twelve stanzas of 'My Love He Was a Travelling Man'. She was well into the seventh and doing badly. She got stuck twice, and when she finally got going again, she had the seventh and the eighth all mixed up.

They were playing Court-the-Princess, and of course Cilla was the Princess. If I knew her at all, she would somehow make the tasks she set her suitors so impossible that no one else would ever get a shot at the throne. The 'courtiers' started to boo and wolf whistle at poor Sasia, and Cilla grandly told her unlucky suitor to go away and return some other day. Then she caught sight of me, and the grand manners crumbled a little.

'What are you doing here?'

'I've come to pay court to the Princess,' I said. 'What else?'

'You're not invited,' Cilla snarled and studied her fingertips in a way that was designed to make it look as if it was simply beneath her dignity to look at me. 'Tell me, Sasia, do you recall us inviting the Shamer's brat?'

Sasia mumbled something, staring at the ground, and I lost my temper.

'You may *think* you're a princess, Cilla,' I said indignantly, 'but you *behave* like a louse!'

Her head came up, and she nearly looked at me. 'I'll give you louse, you—' But she brought herself up short and seemed to reconsider. 'No, I'm sorry,' she resumed. 'Maybe we are being unfair. Dina, if you really want to, you're welcome to play.'

A gasp of disbelief went through the group. I, too, had some difficulty in understanding this sudden change of heart. Generosity was not Cilla's strong suit.

'Do you really mean that? I can play?'

'Wasn't that what you wanted?'

'Yes.'

'All right. Fine. Pay court to me.'

Maybe that was all she wanted – me on my knees in front of her. It galled me a bit, but it had been ages since I had played with anyone but Davin and Melli, and a bit of grovelling seemed a small price to pay. I unbuttoned my cape and threw it across one shoulder to make it look more like a knight's mantle. Sasia tossed me the felt hat without raising her eyes at all.

'O Gentle Princess Lily-white – look with favour upon this Knight,' I intoned, the way I was supposed to.

'I favour no man until he – hath proved his worth for all to see,' replied Cilla, continuing the chant.

'My wit, my skill, my strength, my nerve – command you, for I beg to serve.'

'The trials I demand of thee – are hard indeed and numbered three – of which the first, my knight, shall be . . .' Cilla drew out the last words as if stalling for time, but I could tell by her smile that she had already made up her mind. 'Singing all twelve stanzas of "My Love He Was a Travelling Man" – standing on one leg, blindfolded! Thea, lend her your scarf.'

It is harder than it sounds, standing on one leg with a blindfold on. Luckily the scarf was not too tight and by squinting down the side of my nose I could see the straw of the barn floor and retain some sense of up and down. And I have a much better memory than Sasia.

'My love, he was a travelling man
as fine a tinker as God ever made
he mended every pot and pan
but broke the heart of many a maid . . .'

I was well aware of the giggles and the rustles around me, but I refused to be distracted. Stanza after stanza I sang, ignoring the trembling muscles of the leg I was standing on. When the strain became nearly too much, I concentrated on the sour look on Cilla's face when she had to give up the crown to *me*, and suddenly singing a few more lines became easy. I was just taking a deep breath, ready to start on the twelfth stanza, when it happened.

Something very cold and wet slammed into my face, and instead of air I inhaled a big mouthful of whey. I completely lost my balance and tumbled to the ground, coughing and fighting to breathe. Whey gurgled in my throat, and some of it went up my nose, burning painfully. At first I had no idea what had happened. But once I wrenched off the scarf and saw Cilla standing there with the empty bucket, laughing her head off, things became very clear indeed.

'Get lost, witch brat, and *don't* come back some other day,' said Cilla, nearly choking on her own laughter. She was so busy laughing that she didn't even think about running. And she should have. Never in my life had I been so furious. I needed only one short breath, then I was on my feet, and then on *her*. She keeled over backwards and fell flat on her back, with me astride her chest. I held her face between my hands, and then I took my revenge.

'Look at me, you vain little peahen. **Look into my eyes!**'

She didn't want to. She screamed and wept, trying to close her eyes, but I had her, and I had no intention of letting her go. '**Look at me!**' I hissed once more, and she seemed to lose the will to resist me. The periwinkle blue eyes slid open and stared into mine.

'You are self-centred and spoilt,' I whispered. It was no longer necessary to raise my voice; she could hear my words as clearly as she heard her own thoughts. 'I can't think of a single thing you have ever done for another person. And I know every lousy little trick you have ever used to get your own way. I know how you got that ring you're wearing. I know how you made Sasia give you her favourite blue ribbon. I know how you lied to your brothers to make them beat up Crazy Nate. What had he ever done, other than follow you around because he thought your hair was pretty? Nothing, Cilla. You lied. You are so petty, so mean, so low and wretched that it makes me sick to look at you. I know it all, Cilla. I *know* you.' And I did, I really did. As I sat there on her chest, whispering into her face, I knew every mean thing she had ever done. And though she screamed and kicked and writhed as if she were drowning, there was no way out for her. I forced her to see herself. And I forced her to be ashamed at what she saw.

One of the other girls tried to push me off her, but I only had to turn my head and look at her to make her leap back as though I was spitting acid in her direction.

'You are so wretched, Cilla,' I repeated, slightly louder. 'And if you think any of your court here really like you for your own sake, you are so wrong.'

I got up. Cilla stayed on the floor, weeping so hard that anyone would have thought I had taken a whip to her.

'And you lot,' I continued. 'You're not much better. You who come here to pay court to Princess Cilla, just because you're scared of her, or because you want something from her, or because you like her petty schemes. Go ahead. Play your little games. But do it without me. I have had my fill of you!' I looked around the circle, but the only eyes to meet mine were the eerily-glowing gaze of the turnip lanterns. My anger

9

flickered. This was not at all what I wanted; this was not the ending I had hoped for. But right now it seemed the only thing I could do was walk away from them.

Before I reached the barn doors, one of them swung open, and Cilla's father appeared.

'What do you think you're doing?' he yelled. 'Cilla, what happened?'

Cilla just sobbed on, making no other reply. Then the miller caught proper sight of me, and he wasted no time in deciding who was to blame.

'You devil's spawn, what've you done to her? If you've hurt my Cilla I'll—'

'I barely touched—' but I had no time to finish my sentence. He slapped me so hard across the cheek that the sound echoed in the gloomy space of the barn.

'*Your* kind don't need to *touch*,' he snarled. 'Run on back to your witch of a mother, and if I ever catch you hurting my Cilla again . . . Shamer or no, I'll whip the living daylights out of you, even if I have to pull a sack over your head to do it!'

I could barely stand. My head was buzzing from the slap, and there was a rusty taste of blood in my mouth from where I had bitten my tongue. But I knew better than to ask for sympathy. I straightened and walked out, tall as I could. Trying to look as if I cared not one bit for any of them, not Cilla, not Sasia, nor any of the others, I strode off into the rain without looking back.

Walking the mile or so back home took a while. It took me even longer to steel myself to face my mother. It wasn't just that my green wool cape and my shirt and apron all stank to high heaven from the whey. It was more that – well, I didn't think she would be terribly pleased at what I'd done. I felt so miserable. So lonely. Davin had friends. Melli had friends – everybody thought she was *so* cute. Why was it that I seemed doomed to have no one, other than my family? I ended up in Blaze's stall again; it is amazing how comforting it is to be near a big, warm animal that doesn't care whether you have Shamer's eyes or not. I leaned against the soft, brown neck and cried a bit, as the last of the daylight slowly waned.

A soft glow crept around the edges of the door, and then suddenly Mama was there, holding the lantern we use when we have to go outside at night.

'Dina?' she called softly. 'Why are you standing here in the dark?' She raised the lantern to get a better look at me. 'What happened?'

Lying to my mother is of course a hopeless task. Keeping something secret is nearly as impossible. So I told her most of it, and she guessed the rest. When I was done, she looked at me for a while. She did not scold me. She merely waited until I knew that what I had done was wrong. Then she nodded.

'What you have is a gift,' she said. 'And a power, not to be abused.' She reached into her apron pocket and held something out to me. 'Here. I've been waiting to give you this, and I think the time has come.'

It was a pendant, a round pewter circle decorated with a smaller circle of white enamel, with a still smaller blue circle inside it. It wasn't glittery or beautiful; it had no shiny silver chain or anything, just a round black leather thong fitting like a noose around my neck. But I knew it was a very special thing all the same. Mama had one almost like it, except the inner circle on hers was black rather than blue.

'Why do you want me to have this?'

'Because you're my apprentice now.'

'Your apprentice . . .'

'Yes. Starting tomorrow I shall begin to teach you how to use your gift – and how and when *not* to use it.'

'I don't want to learn to use it,' I said rebelliously. 'What good does it ever do?'

Mama sighed. 'When something has been stolen. Or when some man or woman has hurt another, perhaps even killed . . . that is when they send for the Shamer. There are people in this world who are capable of doing evil without feeling much shame. And there are people so good at hiding their shame, even from themselves, people who can think up a thousand excuses, until they actually believe they have a *right* to hurt, steal, or lie. But when they come face to face with me, they can no longer hide. Not from themselves, nor from others. Most people possess some sense of shame. And if I come across one of the very few who don't . . . well, I can *make* them ashamed if I have to. Because I have a gift which I have learned to use. A rather unusual gift. That you also have.'

'But I don't want it!' It came out on a sob, heartfelt and anguished.

'Oh, child . . . It *is* hard sometimes, and you have been awakened so very early . . . But there is a need for our gift, and I find I cannot wish you did not have it.'

'Even if it means I'll never have any friends? Even if it means no normal person will ever be able to look into my eyes?'

She drew me into her arms, rocking me gently back and forth. 'It isn't that they can't. They just don't want to. You make them remember all the things about themselves that they would rather forget. All the things that they are secretly ashamed of.' She stroked a whey-encrusted lock of hair away from my forehead. 'But you must be patient. Sooner or later you will meet someone who dares to look into your eyes. And then you will be fortunate indeed. For anyone who can meet a Shamer's gaze openly is a very special human being and the best friend you could ever hope for.'

'I don't suppose it will be Cilla,' I said, somewhat gloomily.

Mama laughed. 'No,' she said. 'I don't suppose it will.'

TWO

The Man from Dunark

The wind was stronger now, and the gusts tore at the shutters, making them rattle. Mama had fetched down the big tub and placed it in front of the fireplace in the kitchen, so that I was finally able to get both clean and warm. Washing my sticky hair, I wondered whether we would ever be able to rid my cape of the sickly smell of whey. I had no way of knowing that I would soon have far greater problems.

We ate dinner, and Mama let us roast apples for dessert. Soon a wonderful, sweet and savoury scent filled the kitchen, and I was starting to feel a lot better. Everything was almost back to normal – almost, but not quite. My new pendant hung heavy and strange against my chest, reminding me of my apprenticeship, and of the gift that I would rather not have.

'What happened in the village today?' asked Davin.

'Tell you tomorrow,' I mumbled, drawing Mama's old blue shawl closer around my shoulders, and Davin didn't pester me. He just nodded. One of the good things about Davin – sometimes he actually knows when to be quiet at the right time. Beastie, our big grey wolfhound, was snoring quietly in front of the fire, flat on his side, and Melli had settled herself on Mama's lap.

'Tell the Winter Dragon story,' she begged.

'Not now, Melli.'

'When? Mama, when?'

'*Perhaps* before you sleep. If you behave!'

Mama was carefully penning the labels for the bottles and jars she had filled that day. Apple and pear juice, elderberry wine and rosehip jelly sat in long rows on the kitchen table.

Suddenly Beastie raised his head and gave a short *woof*. There was a knock on the front door. We all sat quite still for a moment except for Beastie, who rolled to his feet and walked stiff-legged towards our small entrance hall. Sighing, Mama put down her pen.

'Easy, Beastie. Davin, get the door.'

Davin handed me his apple stick and got up.

'Why can't they leave us alone at night, at least?' he muttered in annoyance.

'Davin!'

'All right, I'm getting it!'

I sat tensely, half expecting our visitor to be Cilla's dad. But the man entering the hallway was a stranger. Nothing new there – strangers came to see my mother all the time, either to get help for someone who was ill, or, fortunately less often, because they had need of a Shamer.

'Peace to the house,' said the man and cast a wary eye on Beastie, whose head was almost level with his midriff.

'And to you,' my mother replied politely. 'Come on

in. He won't hurt you. Here, sit by the fire and let your clothes dry.'

'I thank you,' he said, throwing back the hood of his dripping wet cloak. 'But there is no time to waste. If you are Melussina Tonerre, that is.' We could see his face now, pale and tense. Strands of his black hair were plastered wetly to his cheeks and forehead, and he looked like a man who had had a hard ride.

'I am,' said my mother briefly. 'And your name?'

'I come not in my own name,' he said, avoiding her gaze. 'I bring you word from the Lawmaster of Dunark.'

I don't think the messenger noticed, but I could see how my mother's narrow shoulders stiffened. Dunark is clear out on the coast, a long ride from Birches, and the Lawmaster would hardly send for her merely for her healing skills. No, they needed a Shamer, and this meant that a crime had been committed.

'Show me, then,' she said quietly.

The man from Dunark loosened a long leather case from his belt and handed it to Mama. I could see Dunark's signet, a raven and a wave, impressed into the bright red wax that sealed the case. Mama broke the seal and drew out a rolled-up scroll. Smoothing it carefully, she placed it close to the lamp, so that she would be able to read it. The soft glow of the oil lamp fell on her smooth, shiny, chestnut hair and on her slim, long hands holding the paper flat. Only her face was left in shadow.

'I see,' she finally said. Her voice had hardened, as it sometimes did when she was trying not to show her feelings. 'Well, I suppose I had better come, then.'

16

'No!' Melli cried out and clutched at Mama's sleeve. 'You promised . . . you promised to tell me the Winter Dragon story.'

She began to cry, and I knew it was not just the dragon story. Melli gets scared when Mama isn't here to tuck her in at night. Especially on a windy night like this one, with all the creaking and the rattling and the cracks of snapping branches in the orchard.

'Hush, baby, hush.' Mama put her arms around Melli and rocked her, much as she had done with me earlier on. 'Davin will tell you the story. And when you wake up tomorrow, I will probably already be home again.'

'He doesn't tell it the way you do!'

'He tells it even better. Come on, sweetie, be a big girl now. Look at Dina. Do you see her crying?'

No, I wasn't crying, but after the day I had had, I *felt* like clinging to my mother and bawling until she promised not to leave us. I didn't, though. I knew Mama had to go; I knew she hated it and would have done almost anything to stay with us, to tuck Melli in and tell her about the Winter Dragon who could not sleep the summer through.

'Come on, Melli,' I said. 'I think your apple is done now. Do you want honey on it?'

Fortunately, Melli has a sweet tooth. 'Lots of honey,' she demanded. 'And jam in the middle!'

I looked at Mama, and she nodded. 'Jam in the middle,' she said. 'But don't forget to clean your teeth afterwards.'

'Can Beastie sleep in my bed?'

'If Dina gives him a good brushing first.' Mama rose, collected her best black shawl from the hook by the stove and tied it around her shoulders. Davin already had her winter cloak ready.

'It's cold,' he said. 'Stay the night if the weather is bad. We can manage.'

'Thanks, my love,' she said. 'I know you can. But I would much rather be home quickly.' She gave him a hug. They were almost the same height now. Same reddish-brown hair. Same slim shape with narrow hands and feet, almost fey-like in their slenderness. Melli and I had more of a square and clumsy look, I thought. Mama called it 'robust' and said that there was a strength in us, and a nearness to the earth. But I would really much rather look like a wood-fey just like her. And who had decided that my hair had to be dull black and coarse, like a horse's tail? If I was to inherit her damned gift, why could I not have some of her prettiness, too? It didn't seem fair.

'Goodnight, my love,' said Mama, kissing Melli's cheek. Melli hugged Mama's neck with a sticky honey paw. She didn't want to let go, but even Melli knew that it was useless to keep complaining.

'Come home right away,' she demanded. 'As quick as you can.'

'As quickly as Blaze can run,' Mama promised, smiling. 'Goodnight, Dina.'

She hugged me, too, and I could feel a slight trembling in her body. I looked at the scroll she was still holding.

'Is it bad?' I asked, softly enough that Melli wouldn't hear.

'It looks bad. But we shall see.'

'Do you want me to come with you? I mean . . . being your apprentice now?'

She shook her head. 'No. You've had enough of a day already. And I want you to start with something less . . . serious.' She touched her lips to my hair. 'Take good care of each other.'

Beastie was already whining and whimpering, begging to be allowed to come, but she seized his long muzzle and looked into his yellow eyes.

'Stay,' she commanded. 'Watch my children for me.'

Our big dog sighed, and his tail hung low, no longer wagging. But he made no attempt to rush after her when the man from Dunark held the door open for my mother and then followed her into the rain and the darkness.

I used a flannel on Melli's honey-sticky hands and face and helped her clean the raspberry seeds from her teeth. Beastie let himself be brushed while Davin told the Winter Dragon story, and after Melli had fallen asleep with Beastie across the foot of the alcove, Davin and I stayed up late, talking. I finally told him the whole stupid story about Cilla.

'Cilla is a selfish little goose,' he said firmly. 'If you shamed her a bit, I'm sure she had it coming. Even her brothers are starting to wise up to some of her tricks.'

Most of the time I am happy to have Davin for an older brother. Not when he is teasing me or bossing me around, of course, but on a night like this, with Mama gone and the wind and the rain and everything, it feels really good to know that he is there and fifteen and almost an adult. The fire had died to embers in the fireplace, and we finally banked it and went to bed, both of us in the same alcove as Melli and Beastie, for company and for warmth. I lay in the darkness listening to the wind as it gradually died down. After a while the rain stopped drumming on the roof and against the shutters, and I thought that if only it would keep dry, Mama might well make the ride back that night. But when we woke the next morning, there was still no sign of her.

THREE

Drakan

We got up the next morning and tried to pretend that everything was just the way it always was. Davin went to pull the shutters back from the windows. Dark grey clouds made the morning dull and sunless, but at least the wind had died down. I fetched water at the pump, stirred up the fire and began to cook the porridge for our breakfast. Melli wanted honey in hers.

'You had plenty of honey yesterday,' I said. 'You'll end up a great big fat honey-bear!'

'I'm not fat,' she said. 'I'm a fine and pretty girl!'

Actually, that was true. There was something soft and fine and shiny about Melli's plumpness, like the feathers on a pigeon or a kitten's fur. Her hair was smooth and shinily reddish-brown like Mama's and Davin's, only perhaps a bit more red than brown. I was the only one in the family who had hair like a horse's.

'That may be,' I said. 'But this honey needs to last us the whole winter.'

'Mama always lets me have a spoonful!'

'That's not true—' I began, but Davin cut me short.

'Let her have the honey.' He was standing by the window, squinting at the sky.

'Davin . . .'

'Don't be so hard on her, Dina.'

'That's not what I meant . . .' I looked at his tired face and the way he held his arms, hugging himself, as if he was freezing. 'Are you all right?'

'I'm fine. But I'm hungry. Is the porridge ready?'

I knew that he was worried about Mama. But I didn't let on. I just ladled out the porridge and gave Melli a large spoonful of honey in her portion.

'The rain stopped during the night,' I said to Davin, quietly.

'Yes,' he said. 'And the wind has died down.'

Our eyes met across the kitchen table, but we did not say what was on our minds: that the weather alone would not have prevented Mama from coming back.

'Here,' I said, handing Davin the honey spoon. 'We could all do with something sweet.'

Shortly after noon, the sun broke through the clouds, and Mama still hadn't made it home. We had fed the goats, the chickens, the pigeons and the rabbits, and collected all the windfall apples and pears. My green cape was nearly dry and had only a slight whiff of whey about it.

'Where's Mama?' asked Melli. 'Why is it taking so long?'

'I don't know, Melli.'

Melli started whimpering. 'I'm scared,' she said. 'Where's Mama?'

'You know what?' I took her hand. 'Davin will take you down to the smithy to visit Ellyn and Rikert. You can play with Sal and Tenna till Mama comes back.'

Melli brightened. 'Do you think Ellyn will make a cake?'

'She often does, doesn't she?' And the smith's wife had a weakness for Melli and her huge, green eyes.

'Won't you come?' Davin asked, but I shook my head.

'It's better that one of us stays here. And better for you if I'm not with you.'

'Rikert isn't afraid of you,' my brother protested.

'Maybe not. But he never looks me in the eye, either. And . . . after what happened yesterday I think I had better stay away for a while.'

'That's no solution,' he objected, looking cross and a bit worried.

'Maybe not. But I'm staying here all the same.'

Once Davin and Melli had set off towards the village, I fetched the fruit basket and sat down on the bench by the woodshed to peel apples. The sunshine and the apple scent made hungry hornets swarm around me, yellow-black and savage. I had to be careful every time I reached for a new apple. Most of the chickens came rushing, to peck and squawk and fight over the peelings. Beastie hunched down in a sunny spot, sighed heavily, and let his big head drop on to his front paws. As a puppy, he used to chase wasps and bees, but he had been stung often enough to leave them alone now.

I dropped another peeled apple into the pot. Suddenly Beastie's head came up, and he made his guarded little *woof.* I shaded my eyes, searching the village road. Surely Davin could not be returning already? Then I heard hoofbeats from the other direction, from the Dunark road. Relief washed through me; Mama was back . . . except now Beastie had leapt to his feet and was barking, loudly and furiously, so that startled chickens scattered all over the yard.

Relief died. Beastie was not what you might call a barkative dog. And under no circumstances would he bark at Mama and Blaze. It had to be a stranger's hoofbeats. Perhaps some passer-by with business in Birches, or someone on his way to the highlands beyond.

A tall black horse appeared round the corner of the goatpen. Its rider, too, looked tall and dark, clad in dark grey leathers and a dark blue cloak. He reined in his horse and cast a glance at Beastie, who was still barking madly. Then he caught sight of me.

'Is this the Shamer's house?' he asked. The black horse snorted, and pawed the ground with one hoof, striking sparks with its iron shoe.

'Yes.' I got up, using my apron to wipe the worst of the apple juice from my hands. 'But the Shamer isn't in right now.'

'No. I know that,' he said and gave a short jerk on the reins. The horse stopped pawing, but I caught hold of Beastie's collar just to be on the safe side. 'You, however, are her daughter, I think?'

'Yes. Dina Tonerre.'

He dismounted and took a few steps towards me. Beastie showed his teeth and jerked at the collar, nearly tearing it from my grasp.

'Easy,' I commanded. 'Sit!'

He sat, reluctantly. The long, grey body was so tense that I could feel him trembling against my thigh. Why was he in such a rage? Was it simply because Mama wasn't here and he felt that he had been left in charge? The stranger stopped and took notice of the set of fangs that Beastie was showing. Then he turned to me again. And although he was now quite close, he looked me straight in the eye.

A curious sort of shock went through me. His eyes were blue, a very dark blue like a midnight sky. A cold and clear one. And his gaze met mine without faltering. *Anyone who can meet a Shamer's gaze openly is a very special human being*, Mama had said. *And the best friend you could ever hope for.* Did this mean that the stranger was a friend? Or might become one? I suddenly looked at him with increased interest. He was beardless, without even the moustache or the goatee that most men wore. His face was smooth, almost like a child's. Everything about it was narrow – the nose, the lips and the chin. It was hard to tell his age, for despite the smoothness there was something about his expression and the look in his eyes that made him seem aeons older than, for instance, Davin or Tork, the miller's eldest.

'I have a message from your mother, Dina,' he said. 'She needs your help.'

The cold sensation I had had when Davin and I looked at each other across the breakfast table was suddenly back, stronger than before.

'Why?' My voice sounded small and lost and frightened.

'She will have to tell you that herself,' he said. 'But if you are not afraid to ride a big horse, we can be there before nightfall. And you're not afraid, are you?'

'No,' I said, though to be frank the black stallion was bigger than any horse I had ever sat on. 'But I have to leave a message for my brother.'

'Your brother? Where is he?'

'At the smithy. It will be a while before he's back.'

I did not even think of hesitating or refusing to come, despite the fact that he was a stranger and Beastie had barked at him. I trusted him. How could I do otherwise, when he stood there, looking me straight in the eye, the way only my family ever could? Perhaps Mama had decided that my apprenticeship would start with whatever had happened in Dunark after all.

I shut Beastie up in the kitchen. As soon as I let go of his collar, he started barking again, jumping up to place his front paws on the edge of the lower door. Hushing him did no good. I washed my hands at the pump. Then I went inside to write the message for Davin. I write neatly. So neatly that Mama often lets me write out the labels for some of the jars and bottles in her pantry — and it certainly makes a difference if the label reads 'Belladonna' or 'Valerian'. Some of the remedies my mother uses are dangerous if given in the wrong dose or to the wrong patient.

'Where are we going?' I shouted to the man waiting patiently outside, still holding the reins of his black horse. 'Dunark?'

'Yes,' he answered. 'Dunark.'

So I wrote my note to Davin, saying that a message

26

had come from Dunark that Mama was still there and needed me. Maybe it was better for him and Melli to stay at the smithy tonight. Love, Dina. I folded the note, addressed it to Davin, and placed it on the kitchen table where he was sure not to miss it. Then I put on my newly washed cape, ordered Beastie into his basket, and returned to the yard.

The black horse looked very big, but the stranger boosted me up as if I weighed nothing at all and settled me with my legs to one side like the grand ladies riding sidesaddle in their long gowns. Of course it looked better than me hiking up my skirts and riding astride, the way I usually did, but it was also a lot more difficult. I felt as if I was about to slide off the whole time. The stranger mounted behind me, put his arm around my waist in a firm grip, and still managed to control the horse one-handedly and with total ease.

'I still don't know your name,' I said nervously.

'Drakan,' he replied, not deigning to tell me whether that was a first or a last name. Then he prodded the horse into a canter, and I had my hands full just staying on. But as the black stallion's long strides brought us further and further down the road to Dunark, I could hear Beastie still, barking and barking as if he would never stop.

FOUR

The Dragon Pit

Dunark was an old fortress which had gradually become a town. It sat on top of an enormous pile of rock, towering over the flat and muddy wetlands around it. There was a story about an ancient giant, Dun, who in a fit of rage had grabbed an entire mountain-top and flung it at a taunting mermaid. The mountain-top had landed slightly short of its mark, creating the Dun Rock, which now rose in front of us, black and square and forbidding.

'Have you been here before?' asked Drakan, who had been mostly silent for the entire trip.

'Once,' I said. 'With my mother. But we came in through *that* gate . . .' I pointed at Eastgate, which was where travellers arrived if they followed the old Dunark Road.

'This is quicker,' he said. He had left the road a while ago, guiding the leggy black stallion along a much less travelled path. The horse had had to leap or wade through several sluggish canals, which had not been easy with two people on its back. I sincerely hoped

28

Drakan's assurance that this was the quicker way was true; my bottom and my back hurt incredibly from the long ride in my awkward sideways position.

The gate we finally came to was much smaller than Eastgate – not much more than a man-and-horse-sized opening barred by a metal grille. Thistles and nettles crowded the track, and the grille looked depressingly rusty. Did *anyone* ever come this way? But it turned out a guard was actually waiting to let us in.

'All quiet?' Drakan asked.

'Yes. So far.'

Drakan nodded, then spurred the black stallion forward, into a narrow passage between old, crumbling fortress walls – a passage so narrow that the toes of my boots brushed against the brickwork more than once. In places it was so overhung with bridges and galleries that it became more of a tunnel, and I wondered at the stallion, who walked there so calmly. Horses were meant for fields and open plains, not cramped and shadowed pits like this one. I hated it. When the sky was visible at all, it was just a narrow ribbon of blue somewhere impossibly high above our heads, and though the afternoon sun gilded the tall merlons, it never reached all the way down into this dank and gloomy canyon. Yet the stallion climbed steadily upwards, towards the top of the Dun Rock. The time I went to Dunark with my mother, I had been a bit frightened by the teeming swell of people, carts and beasts seemingly all trying to get through Eastgate at once. This was completely different; on our whole journey from the guarded gate to the fortress at the top of the rock, we met not a single soul.

Yet somehow, that was not very reassuring either.

Finally we reached yet another gate and yet another guard, who greeted Drakan and let us into a yard big enough to breathe in. A groom came to take the reins of the black horse, and I slithered uncertainly to the ground. My knees threatened to buckle, but Drakan held my elbow until my legs became a bit steadier.

'This way, Dina,' he said and guided me towards some stone steps, still holding my arm. I was loath to give up my glimpse of the sky so soon, but down the steps we went, and into a long cellar passage. Then down another stair, through a door, along another passage . . . I could get lost in this place, I thought, with no trouble at all. Finally Drakan came to a halt in front of the bars of another rusty iron gate.

'Wait here a moment,' he ordered, taking a key from his belt and thrusting it into the cumbersome lock. He slipped through the gate, locked it again behind him, and disappeared from sight.

I waited obediently. This cellar smelled strange – of animals, but also of something else, something rotten and unpleasant. Perhaps we were close to the stables? But horses didn't smell like this. I tried to peer through the gate but could see nothing in the dimness except more iron bars and a weak hint of daylight at the end – or was it just a torch? There was a clang, a thud, and some peculiar hissing and dragging noises. Then Drakan reappeared, striding hurriedly. He opened the gate to let me through, and I saw that he had armed himself with a spear that was taller than he was.

'What is this place?' I asked nervously.

'The Dragon Pit,' he said tersely. 'Stay close to me and you'll be quite safe.'

'*The Dragon Pit?*' I could not believe it. There were rumours about the Pit of Dunark Castle, and about the monsters in it: huge scaly worms capable of swallowing a grown man in a few gulps. A ten-year-old girl would be just a little titbit to them.

'Calm yourself. I'm used to handling them. And you do want to see your mother, don't you?'

'Yes . . . but, isn't there some other way? Do we have to go past—'

'Yes. And come on, I just fed them, so that they would have other things to occupy them while we cross the Pit.'

He gave me no time for further objections. He simply seized my arm and pulled me along through the next gate and into the open.

I came to an abrupt halt when I saw the first dragon. It was not as big as I had feared, for in my nightmares dragons were bigger than houses. But it was something much worse than that. It was *real*. Not quite as tall as a horse, but almost three times as long. Scaled like a serpent. Fat, waddling legs with huge claws that clicked against the rubble. Yellow eyes and a long, flat skull. And a maw full of fanged teeth, from which dangled a bloody mess that used to be the hind leg of a calf. A bit further off five more monsters were busy ripping the rest of the bullock apart. And we had to walk past all of them!

'Now, Dina. Quietly and calmly,' Drakan said and started forward without letting the nearest dragon out of his sight. It opened its jaws somewhat and hissed at him, and a heavy rotten stench washed over us. I clung to Drakan's arm, and my heart beat so that I could barely hear anything else. But the dragon apparently did not want to relinquish the meat in its mouth in favour of a taste of girl. It watched us sullenly with gleaming yellow eyes while we walked past it, less than three dragons' lengths away. No sound had ever been sweeter to me than the clang of the gate swinging shut between me and that creature.

'Why are they here?' I asked. 'Who would willingly keep such monsters *in his house?*'

'Don't you like them?' Drakan was still watching the nearest yellow-eyed reptile. 'Can't you see that they have their own kind of beauty? Strong, lithe and dangerous. And you can trust them – trust them to be true to their natures – always and completely. Not much different, really, than your own snappish guard dog.'

'They're nothing like Beastie!' I was outraged at the thought. Beastie, who liked me to scratch his belly and his ears; Beastie, who was a big, warm, cuddly bedmate for us when Mama was away . . .

'Not many people see it,' Drakan said. 'But the beauty is there all the same. And as guards they are better than the most vicious pack of hounds you can find me.'

The yellow-eyed monster flung back its head and swallowed its meat. Almost a quarter of a calf, hair and hide and hoof and all, gone in one mouthful. You could see its neck swell with it, a lump moving slowly towards the belly of the beast, making the greeny-grey scales shift and ripple, almost like water. At least the calf was already dead, I thought. What would it be like to be swallowed alive?

Drakan turned away from his 'guard dogs', with some reluctance, it seemed.

'Your mother is waiting,' he said. 'We had better hurry.'

It needed yet another key to get us through the last gate, and then we were inside a whitewashed cellar vault, lit only by thin slivers of daylight entering through three peepholes high above us. The vault itself sported two doors, but Drakan led me up a flight of stairs, along a short passage to a third door, which he opened.

After the dimness of the vaults and the Pit, the light in this room was nearly blinding. Warm yellow evening sun poured in through a large circular window and made the woman standing in front of it appear only as a dark form. But it was a form I knew.

'Mama . . .'

She turned around. The light behind her was so brilliant that I couldn't see the expression on her face. But the sharpness in her voice was unmistakable.

'Dina! What are you doing here, girl?'

FIVE

Bloody Deeds

I felt completely lost. I had come all the way from Birches to Dunark. I had ridden for several hours on the biggest horse I had ever been on. I had crossed the Dragon Pit, passing six monsters capable of swallowing a child in a single gulp. I was tired and sore and frightened. And all of that because Drakan had said that my mother needed me.

'You said . . . he said . . . he said that you'd said . . .' My throat stopped working. I was on the verge of tears. But my mother was no longer watching me. She was staring at Drakan as if she meant to burn a hole in him.

'What is the meaning of this?' Her voice was so cold that the frost on it was nearly visible.

'I thought we might talk about the terrible crimes of Mesire Nicodemus. Again.'

'I have told you: he didn't do it.'

'How can you be so certain? Maybe the Shamer ought to speak to him one more time.'

'What good would that do? I was with him for hours. I have seen every shameful secret in his soul. He has his

34

flaws. Human flaws. But this . . . this inhuman deed he has not done. I swear it, by my word as Shamer. Find me another suspect and I'll see what I can do. But if you have no other possible killer, let me go home. My children have already waited far too long.'

'Mesire Nicodemus was found with the dagger in his hand and the blood of the victims on his hands and clothes. He may have done it in a drunken rage; he may have been barely himself at the time. But most certainly, he did it. He did it, though he may not *remember* doing it.'

'He did *not* do it. There would have been marks on his soul, and there were none.'

'Surely such marks may yet appear?'

My mother stood silent for a moment, straight and edged like a spear. 'And what exactly does Mesire Drakan mean by that?' Her voice was clear as glass and just as sharp. If Beastie had heard that tone of voice, he would have hidden under the bed, whimpering.

'Medama Tonerre. All the evidence points to him. He claims to remember nothing, but I think the Shamer can make him recall his guilt.'

'Not if he is innocent.'

'An old man. A four-year-old boy. A woman and her unborn child. Four lives, Medama. Is it so strange that he clings to forgetfulness?'

'A man cannot be brought to remember something he has not done.' My mother still had not moved, but her voice was less crystalline.

'I was there for the arrest, Medama. Shall I tell you what the Duchessa's bedroom looked like? Shall I tell you how many times he had stabbed her, and where? She used to be so beautiful, Medama. But not any more.'

'Guard your tongue, Mesire,' said my mother, angry and outraged. 'The child . . .' She waved a hand in my direction.

'Medama is right, it is no tale for children. But she was my cousin's wife. And *her* child had to do more than merely listen. Four years old. It will be very, very hard for me to forget this. And I want . . .' his voice went hoarse with passion, 'I want that monster to *remember* what he has done. Is that too much to ask of justice?'

'But I tell you—'

'Yes. I've heard. But if the Shamer is really so very certain of her judgement . . . then surely there can be no harm in letting the Shamer's daughter spend the night in the monster's cell. Pardon me. In the cell of this *innocent* man.' The word came out dripping with acid, as if he could barely make himself pronounce it.

My mother took an involuntary step forwards, putting herself between me and Drakan. 'Is that why . . .'

'That is why I fetched her, yes. It is so easy to judge among strangers, isn't it? Guilty or innocent, it doesn't really touch you. All right. Let him out of his cage, if you are so certain of his innocence. But first, leave your daughter with him for one night.'

'So you would use a child—'

'She is far older than my nephew had the chance to be.' He turned away from her. 'Think it over for a while,' he said, moving towards the door. 'I will return to hear your answer in an hour's time.'

'Wait!' She caught hold of his arm, turning him to face her. '***Are you not ashamed—***' she began. And the look was *that* look, and the voice *that* voice, the one that made thieves and murderers cringe with guilt and ask for a well-deserved punishment. But Drakan met her gaze without flinching.

'No,' he said firmly. 'I am not ashamed in the least.'

SIX

Even or Uneven

The door slammed, and we could hear Drakan's steps receding down the stairs. Where was he going? Would he have to pass the dragons again?

'Mama, are they real dragons?'

'Dragons?'

'Out there in the Pit.'

'Oh, those. I don't really know, I hardly saw them. It was dark and I was in the middle of a troop of guards with torches. But there was a strange smell, and the men were scared. Did you go that way? Just him and you?'

I nodded. It wasn't that I hadn't been listening; I did hear all that about people having been killed and about the man that Drakan said had done it. But the dragons – those I had *seen*. Their smell still lingered in my nostrils. I was more scared of them than of – what was his name – that Nicodemus person whom Drakan called a monster.

'Come here. Your braid has come undone.'

My braid is always coming undone. That's just the way it is when you have hair like a horse's tail. But

Mama's hands moved more gently than they usually did as she undid my hair, combed it with her fingers, and braided it again.

'Were you scared of them?' she asked.

'They were ugly. Scaly all over, like snakes. And they tore a calf apart in *seconds*.'

Mama tightened the leather thong as firmly as she could. I knew it would come undone again anyway, possibly even before Drakan returned. She stood behind me for a little while, resting her cheek against my hair.

'Don't be frightened,' she said. 'He is angry because I won't say what he wants me to say. But he won't hurt you. He wouldn't dare.'

'Mama . . . he looked you straight in the eye.'

She sighed, and put her arms around me. 'Yes. I am not quite sure what that means. He certainly isn't ashamed. And Mesire Nicodemus – the one they say did it – he is ashamed of many things, but not of this. And he is so very young, Dina; seventeen, just a few years older than Davin. They don't believe me, Drakan and the Lawmaster, but I am certain of his innocence.'

'Who is it he . . . who was it that was killed?'

'The Castellan himself – old Lord Ebnezer. And his daughter-in-law Adela, who was the widow of his oldest son, the one that was killed by robbers six months ago. And his grandson, Bian.'

'But why would anyone kill them?'

'Mesire Nicodemus is Lord Ebnezer's youngest son. They say he wanted to marry Adela after his brother's death but that the Castellan would not permit it. They say he drank himself into a fury and killed the Castellan, and then Adela for refusing him, and the child . . . the child perhaps only for having been there and having seen it all. It looks so obvious. They found him raving drunk in the antechamber, covered in blood and with the dagger still in his hand. He remembers nothing and could give them no explanation. The Lawmaster was certain of his case. But I am just as certain of mine. He did not do it.'

She put her hands on my shoulders and turned me around, so that she could see my face, almost as she had just done with Drakan. She was pale, and there were purplish shadows under her eyes. She might not have had any sleep at all since leaving us to ride away into last night's rain and wind.

'What Drakan wants me to do is a terrible thing. Making a man believe that he has done such an inhuman deed *if he hasn't* . . . that would be a crime almost as cruel as those horrible murders. Do you understand that?'

I nodded. 'But *could* you? Could you make him believe that?'

She let go of me abruptly, her face suddenly very cold and strict. 'Why do you ask?'

'If I am to be your apprentice, shouldn't I know what a Shamer is capable of?'

'I might be able to do it. Or I might not. But I would never, ever try. Do you understand? I would never shame myself so. And that is why . . .' She put her hands on my shoulders again. 'Dina, if he is serious about his threat . . . then you must be brave, and trust me. Nicodemus is a young man, barely more than a boy, ashamed of all sorts of ordinary things – and *not* the monster they want to make him.'

When Drakan returned, the sun had nearly set, and the sky outside the circle window was streaked with pink and golden clouds. Mama and I sat on the window seat playing Even and Uneven with a few coins from my mother's purse. At first he remained in the doorway, watching us.

'Even.' My mother made her guess as if not realizing that Drakan was in the room.

'Uneven,' I said, showing her the three coins in my hand.

I think this made him angry. He strode into the room, slamming the door behind him.

'Well?' he said.

'Well, what?' my mother inquired, and this did not please him any better.

'I await your answer, Medama. Where is the Shamer's daughter to spend the night?'

'In her bed, I hope. Mesire Drakan, this charade has gone on long enough. I have every sympathy with the anger and the horror this crime has engendered. But having done my Shamer's duty, I wish to go home.'

'No. I do not play games, Medama. This is no act. I believe we can condemn him without the Shamer's say, but I want him to *know* that he is guilty. Dina, come here.'

I cast an uncertain look at my mother, but the twilight made it difficult to read her expression.

'Leave the girl be. She has done nothing wrong.'

41

'Neither had Bian,' said Drakan in a low voice and put his hand on my arm. 'Come on. We're leaving.'

I pulled back. It is one thing to be brave in daylight, but now that night was coming, I wanted to be with my mother. But Drakan had other plans. He pulled me to my feet with a grip so hard that it made my breath whistle between my teeth.

'Well?' he repeated. 'This can stop any time. The decision is yours, Medama.'

Mama raised her head. 'Go with him, Dina,' she said quietly. 'Remember what I said. Nicodemus will not harm you.'

I was still frightened. But my mother looked so proud and calm that I wanted her to be proud of me as well.

'It really isn't necessary to hold me, Mesire,' I said in my coolest, most polite tone of voice. 'I am perfectly capable of walking on my own.'

Mama smiled. Drakan looked as if a flea had bitten him. But he released my arm, and I walked with even, measured steps to the door and through it, without looking back.

SEVEN

The Monster

The smell was almost as bad as the one in the Dragon Pit. He had vomited several times, and the straw covering the floor of the cell had been none too clean to begin with.

'If I am to sleep in there, I want it cleaned,' I declared.

'Drakan said—' began one of the guards, but then I caught his eye. And I felt nearly certain that Mama would think it all right to use the gift now.

'*This is no way to treat a human being.*' I tried to sound exactly like Mama when she used the Shamer's voice, and I think I succeeded, at least a little bit. He ducked his head and would no longer look at me.

'We can sweep out the straw,' he said. 'And get you some water. But I can't lay my hands on clean straw at this hour of the night.'

'Water, then. *Hot* water, at least two buckets full. And soap.'

He nodded without raising his head. 'Karman, get a broom,' he called to one of the others. 'And you. Get that water!'

I stepped up to the bars to get a look at the man who was to be my cellmate. Mesire Nicodemus lay on a brick ledge meant to serve as the prisoner's bed. He had his face turned to the wall and did not look up, not even when Karman came back with the broom, and the door was opened. While Karman swept the dirty straw from the cell, four armed men guarded the prisoner with lowered spears, but he moved not a muscle.

'See to the rest yourself,' said Karman bitterly. 'Me, I get sick just looking at that unnatural creature. This way, Medamina.' He placed the buckets in the cell and bowed ironically, as though I were some fine lady on her way to a grand ball. I walked past him into the cell, and they locked the door behind me.

He lay curled up on his side, face to the wall. His shirts had once been of the finest white linen, embroidered in blue and gold. Now one shoulder was torn and the cloth was spattered with huge maroon stains. His long dark hair was drawn back in a ponytail, partially undone. I could not see his face.

'Mesire Nicodemus?' I said, hesitantly.

At first he seemed not to have heard. Then he slowly turned around and dragged himself up to sit on the ledge, hunched and slouching. Seventeen, my mother had said, and he looked both younger and older now, I thought. His expression was somehow both hardened and lost, and his face was swollen and battered around the jaw, nose, and left cheekbone. They had been rough on him, the guards.

'A *girl*?' he muttered in a tone of wonder. 'What are you doing here? Who are you?'

'Dina Tonerre.' And then our eyes met.

'Oh, God,' he whispered, hiding his face in his hands. 'Oh, God. Not again. Please, Medamina, please . . . just leave.'

'I can't. They locked the door.' I tried not to let my voice shake, but I think it did anyway. 'I am to . . . stay here all night.'

Surprised, he glanced at me, but looked away quickly. 'Why?'

'Something to do with my mother and Drakan.'

It was so natural for him to look at the person he was talking to that he kept forgetting that he would really rather not meet my eyes. But every time he did, he cringed as if it hurt him.

'Your mother . . . that would be the Shamer, I suppose?' He put a hand over his face again.

'Yes.'

'You have her eyes.'

'I know.' And then I really noticed his hands. They had not let him wash. Dried blood remained encrusted at the knuckles, between his fingers, and under his nails. *They had not let him wash.* If my mother was right, and he was innocent, then . . . then they had made him sit here with blood on his hands, his father's blood, Adela's blood and the little boy's blood . . . one whole night and one whole day he had been left like this, with his dead family's blood on his hands.

Suddenly something was far more important than clean floors. I grabbed one bucket and placed it in front of him and handed him the rough yellow cake of soap that they had given us.

'Here,' I said. 'So you can wash.'

For a moment, he just sat there. Then his shoulders began to tremble, so that I was afraid that he might be about to cry. He held his hands out, spreading his fingers, and the hands were shaking. But he forced himself to face me for a moment. His eyes were almost as dark a blue as Drakan's, but the whites were so reddened that it hurt to look at them.

'Thank you,' he said. 'I had no idea that the Shamer's daughter could be so . . . merciful.'

He seized the soap the way a starving man would clutch at a loaf of bread. He scrubbed his hands and arms over and over again, then tore the shirt from his body and washed his chest and back and even his hair, though it made him shiver with cold. One whole side of his chest was bruised and darkened, like Rikert's had once been after the miller's huge cart-horse had kicked him. He had nothing that he could use for a towel, since he refused to touch the blood-spattered shirt again. I took off my apron and offered it to him.

'Thank you,' he said again, once more painfully forcing himself to meet my eyes. 'You'll be cold,' I mumbled when he kicked the shirt into a corner of the cell, as far away as possible.

'It hardly matters,' he said. 'I doubt they'll keep me alive long enough for me to get sick.'

'My mother has told them that she knows you're innocent.'

'Has she?' He studied his hands with great care. 'Then she knows more about the matter than I do.' He looked at me again, as if believing that it would hurt less if he

46

kept at it long enough. 'And how can she call me innocent when she knows . . .' His voice broke, but he continued all the same. 'When she knows everything *else*. Every other thing I've ever done. Or not done. Every shameful, petty, pathetic misdeed. The people I've hurt. Every good act I was too cowardly to do. Everything I've taken from others and everything I was too petty, scared or greedy to give . . . No, Medamina, I may be a lot of things, but I am certainly not *innocent*!' He spat out the word as though it hurt his mouth to say it. 'But still I would not have thought . . . I did not think I could ever hurt Adela. And the boy. God. Bian, who . . . no, I did not think I was capable of that, however drunk I was.'

'My mother says you didn't do it. And she is rarely wrong.'

His eyes stared vacantly at something – visions, ghosts, memories – that was invisible to me. 'I don't remember,' he said tonelessly. 'I can't remember doing it, but I can't remember *not* doing it, either. And it has been rather hard to forget that I had their blood on my hands.'

I studied him for a moment. '*I* don't think you did it,' I pronounced with all the certainty I could muster.

'You're a child,' he said. 'Children think well of everyone.' But the emptiness left his eyes. 'What are you *doing* here?' he asked. 'Has Drakan lost his mind completely, to let a little girl into a condemned man's cell?'

'I am nearly eleven years old,' I said with some irritation. 'And you are not a condemned man. Not while my mother says you're innocent. And that . . . is actually why I am here. Drakan thinks he can make her change her mind.'

'And can he?'

I shook my head, smiling. 'He doesn't know my mother very well.'

I took my little belt knife, hardly longer than my finger, and started to cut slivers off the soap into the other bucket of water. I then beat the water frothy with my hand and used the broom for a mop. Nicodemus retreated to the ledge, pulling up his feet so as not to be in the way. Probably the Castellan's son had never actually held a broom in his hands.

It was now completely dark outside, as far as one could see through the tiny peephole that was also the cell's only source of daylight and fresh air. In the corridor outside an oil lamp had been hung, casting a yellow, flickering light into the cell. From the guardroom at the end of the passage came occasional loud voices – judging from the roars of triumph and accusation it seemed that the guards were playing some sort of card game.

'Medamina . . .' said Nicodemus.

'I'm not really used to titles,' I interrupted. 'Please call me Dina; at least I'll know who you're talking to.'

'Dina,' he said. 'Then you must call me Nico. All my friends do. *Did*. But what I wanted to say was . . . There's really no need for you to stay here all night. Call the guards. I'm sure Drakan merely wanted to . . . unsettle your mother a bit.'

I shook my head. 'I don't think he is about to give up that easily. And anyway . . . if I call the guards now, I've lost. And I hate losing. Besides, I'm not afraid of you.'

He gave a brief snort of laughter. 'So I've noticed. But still. This place is cold and inconvenient. And there are – well, *rats*.' He said the last bit as if expecting me to raise my skirts and leap on to the ledge, screaming for the guards. Perhaps that was how the girls he knew would have behaved.

'There are rats under the floor of the stable at home,' I said calmly. 'Beastie – that's our dog – he kills them when he can, but they're not easy to get rid of. Besides, you're much colder than I am.' Actually he was shaking all over, I could see. I took off my cape. 'Here. Try this. It's much too small, I know, but it might still warm you a little.'

'That wasn't – I can't—'

'Take it. You can give it back later, when you're a bit warmer.'

He took it. It reached around his shoulders, barely, if one buttoned only the lowermost of the three horn buttons. And as it was cut to fall to my knees, at least it covered most of his bare chest.

A little while later there were steps in the passage, and one of the guards came to unhook the lamp outside the cell.

'Bedtime,' he called. 'And you, Monster Nicodemus!'

'Yes, what about me?' Nico said tiredly.

'This is all Drakan's idea, not mine. But I promise you, Monster, that if you lay a finger on that girl . . .'

'I'll do her no harm.'

'No. You won't. Because you know that if you do, I'll personally break every bone in your body *before* they chop off your head.' He glared at Nico, then nodded briefly in my general direction. 'Goodnight, Medamina Tonerre. Just give a shout if he acts up. We're just down the passage.'

'Goodnight, Guardmaster. And thank you, but that won't be necessary.'

He muttered something and went away, taking the lantern with him. The cell became almost completely dark. A very thin, pale sliver of moonlight penetrated the peephole, and that was all.

'I'll sleep on the floor,' said Nico. 'You take the ledge.'

'Don't be silly.' I tried to sound just like Mama when she becomes impatient with Melli. 'There is plenty of room on the ledge for both of us, and it will be far warmer.'

'But you can't – I mean, you had better not touch me.' He sounded almost panicky.

'Don't be silly,' I repeated. 'You're not a monster, are you? You won't harm me.' And before he could come up with any more objections, I sat down next to him and leant against his shoulder.

His whole body jerked. His breath came and went in a hiccupy gasp. And perhaps it was the darkness. And perhaps it was because no one had touched him in kindness since the bloodbath in Adela's room. Or perhaps it was simply that he had come to the end of his strength. He began to cry, helplessly and uncontrollably, shaking all over, and his arms wrapped themselves around me and clung, clung to me as if I was the only thing that could save him from drowning.

'Some monster you are,' I whispered. 'How is anyone supposed to be afraid of you?'

After a while his shoulders stopped shaking and his breathing became easier. But he still held on to me, and it was nice to be held, for it had been a long and frightening day. My own breath slowed to a sleepier rhythm and I yawned. He moved a little further up the ledge, so that I could rest more comfortably.

'So strange,' he said softly, into the darkness. 'You are your mother's daughter. And yet . . . her eyes tear me apart and make me feel like the sorriest beast to ever crawl upon this earth. While you . . .' He sighed, a gusty little breath of air against my cheek. 'You make me believe that I might be innocent after all.'

EIGHT

Peace in a Bottle

I woke some while later, I don't really know how long.
The skinny stripe of moonlight had moved, but not a
lot. Nico was breathing deeply and steadily, but I didn't
think he was asleep. Then it came again, the sound that
had woken me up – footsteps outside in the passage.
The dancing light of a lantern flickered across the wall.

It was Drakan.

'Nico,' he called softly. 'Nico, are you awake?'

Nico eased himself out from under me, carefully so as
not to disturb me – he hadn't realized that I was no
longer asleep. And I kept my eyes shut and pretended
to be, in order not to interrupt anything. Drakan had
called him Nico – and Nico had said that only his
friends did that.

'I'm awake,' he said.

'The Shamer still claims that you are innocent. She is
absolutely adamant. And so I thought . . . perhaps I had
better come and talk to you myself. I hardly know
what to believe any more.'

Nico slowly got to his feet. Watching through my

52

lashes, I could see that he was moving stiffly – lying still in the chill of the night had done his bruised and battered body no good.

'I'm glad you came,' he said softly. 'But there's not much I can tell you. I remember nothing until you and the guards shook me awake and I saw . . . everything.'

'But before that? You must have had a reason to go to Adela's rooms.'

Nico shook his head. 'I really don't know. Marten had come up with that silly barrel race, and we were yelling our heads off and drinking too much, and I lost three silver marks to Ebert and nearly killed myself thinking I could stay balanced on the barrel with him inside it . . . but you were there. You saw it. Better than I, probably.'

'The last thing I saw of you, you were sitting on top of a haystack, having declared it your kingdom. It was late in the afternoon, and you were very, very drunk.'

'I don't even remember that.'

'You were singing at the top of your lungs, earsplittingly off key, and when Ebert wanted to make you stop, you held him off with a pitchfork. Finally you collapsed and started snoring, and we carried you off to your rooms. But you must have revived and drunk even more, there were that many bottles in your room. And then you must have gone to Adela's rooms. Nico, you *must* have.'

'I don't remember . . .' Nico whispered, clutching the bars of the door.

'Try,' Drakan demanded, harshly. '*Try*. You are climbing the stairs in the west wing – you must have come up the Secret Steps or someone would have seen you – you're walking along the hall, you knock . . . or what? What did you want to see her for? Does she open the door? Or do you just walk right in? And *why* have you brought your dagger? Think, damn you. *Remember.*'

Nico made a sound, a sort of moan. 'I can't. Do you think I haven't tried? I've thought of nothing else, how could I? But it's gone. All gone. *I can't remember.*'

'I thought perhaps now that you had sobered up . . .'

'No. It's still just a blank.'

'Nico, I . . . really hope that the Shamer is right. You're my cousin. And my friend. And I have lost enough relatives.'

'I've begun to think that perhaps . . . perhaps I really didn't do it. I still can't explain what I was doing in Adela's rooms. But something has changed inside me. Now I think that an explanation does exist. All I have to do is look for it . . .'

Drakan considered his cousin carefully. 'Good luck in your search, then. And here. A small reconciliation gift.' He held out a leather-covered bottle. 'You must have the meanest hangover in the universe.'

Nico looked at the bottle but did not take it. 'I don't think the kind of answers I am looking for can be found in that,' he finally said.

Drakan smiled faintly. 'Answers, no. But perhaps . . . peace. Take it. Keep it. Call it a peace offering. From me to you. I'm sorry I acted . . . like I did. But I was beside myself.'

'With good reason.' Nico accepted the bottle. 'And

whatever the outcome . . . I am glad, cousin, that you came down here.' He uncorked the bottle and took a sniff at the contents. 'And not just because of this, though the bouquet is promising.'

Drakan waved away his thanks. 'And the girl? Was she very frightened?'

Nico gave another of his short laughs. 'Hardly. She is her mother's daughter.'

Drakan sighed. 'I was so furious at that Shamer. I didn't believe that she knew what she was doing. But now . . . I suppose she might as well have her daughter back. At least you will have that ledge to yourself.' He unhooked the lantern again. 'It might be a while – I have to find the key first. Let the wine warm you up meanwhile.' He walked back along the passage, taking the light with him. Nico remained at the door, sniffing the wine.

'I need it,' he finally muttered, taking a swallow. 'Just a little drink.'

Drakan took his time. Nico's little drink became five, then ten.

'Don't you think you've had enough?' I asked.

'Is that any of your business?' Nico demanded. Not really angry, but certainly annoyed.

'You said it yourself – you won't find the answers in there.'

'Little Miss Prim. Nose in the air, just like your mother.' His voice had already lost some of its distinction, had become blurred and somehow soggy. Ten draughts – eleven now – could he really become drunk so soon on so little?

'Nico . . . hold on a minute. Isn't that stuff working a little too quickly?'

'Not quick enough for me. Not nearly. Life is short and you're such a long time dead.' He took yet another swallow. 'A very long time dead,' he said. And then he peered at the bottle with some thoughtfulness. 'You're right,' he said, rubbing his eyes with the back of his hand. 'It really – does work – a lot more quickly – than it usually does . . .'

'Give it to me,' I said, reaching for the bottle.

'Mine,' he muttered, just like Melli does when you want to take something away from her. 'My bottle. *My* death. Drakan gave it to me.'

I placed myself squarely in front of him, in the middle of the stripe of moonlight.

'Look at me,' I said.

'Not again,' he pleaded, so softly that it was barely more than a whimper.

'***Look at me.***'

He slowly raised his eyes to mine. Not because I forced him to, but of his own free will. Whatever was wrong with him, that was one kind of courage he did not lack. The moonlight fell on one side of his face, leaving the other in shadow, and his eyes were so dark that they looked like caverns. But somewhere in those caverns was a light, a tiny glimmer of light. I stared into that light, and something weird happened to my head. Images started to form in the darkness. *A slender dark-haired boy on his seventh birthday, watching from the shadows as his brother wins the race astride a sweaty chestnut horse shining like copper in the sunlight. People clapping and cheering, a smiling Castellan punching the older boy in the shoulder, proud of his heir, his brave boy. The dark-haired boy, a little older now, face thrust into the cobbles in the Arsenal Court, his brother holding him down, yelling, 'Give up yet? Huh, Nico? Little Nicola, do you yield?' Thirteen-year-old Nico in front of the mirrors in the fencing hall, sabre raised, dripping with sweat and trembling from the strain, as the swordmaster hits him with his stick every time he lowers his arm or slumps his shoulders. Nico, fourteen, staring across a wide dark canal, then making the decision: flinging the sword away from him, as hard as he can. The slender blade glitters, dropping into the black water with hardly a splash, and as he watches the sabre disappear into the weedy depths, a deep sense of relief. A man, hitting his nearly grown son again and again, with fists, with his stick, with the flat of his sword, again and again, pounding the lesson into him: 'A man is nothing without his sword!' Nico, meeting his brother's wife for the first time, staring into green eyes and hair like copper gold, whispering into his pillows at night and his horse's neck by day, 'Adela, Adela, Adela!' yet knowing it is hopeless, and so, getting drunk, clowning, making the hall ring with laughter, men patting his back and encouraging him to drink still more, egging him on to wilder capers, only two people not sharing in the laughter, his furious father at the head of the table and Adela, who bends her head, letting the fall of red-gold hair hide her pity. Other girls, girls he feels less than nothing for, except that they prove someone can like him, someone can love him . . . Drinking, clowning, dropping, getting up to drink and clown some more. And caring not at all what happens to him or to anyone around him except two people, the furious father, the pitying Adela. Caring not at all. And then the darkness was back,* and the moonlight, the moonlight which glittered in the trail of tears on Nico's cheeks.

'You are a merciless mirror, Medamina,' he whispered. 'But the image is very clear.'

There was a pain in my head, somewhere behind the eyes. But I knew that what I had seen was true, and that he had seen it with me.

He had dropped the bottle, and the remains of the wine spread in a pool across the floor, unnoticed. He turned his back on me, fumbling for the empty bucket. Kneeling, he thrust a finger into his mouth until he gagged, and then threw up. I swallowed. And swallowed some more. When Melli and Davin were ill, I sometimes threw up along with them in sheer sympathy. I did not dare go near him or try to help him, for fear of ending up with my own head over the bucket.

Finally he stopped retching. Taking a mouthful of water from the other bucket, he rinsed his mouth. Then he stumbled to the ledge, grabbed my apron which we had been using for a pillow, and dried his face with it.

'I'm sorry,' he said. 'I know it's not a pleasant sight, but at least it's effective.' He leaned back against the wall, swallowing. His face was gleaming with sweat. 'God, I feel sick. The good Lord's just punishment for all drunks.' His breathing was coming hard and fast now; I could see his chest rising and falling at a much too rapid rate.

'Mama always tells us to keep our breathing slow and calm. It will make you feel better.'

'Probably. Your mother is a wise woman.' He did his

best to slow his breathing, but it didn't seem to do much good. He got halfway to his feet, then fell back against the ledge again. 'I think I'll have to lie down for a little while,' he said.

I stayed where I was, midway between the window and the door. My own nausea had subsided, but I felt suddenly shy. Seeing the images inside somebody else's head . . . it was strange. Like seeing them with no clothes on, only worse. Staring right into their secrets, knowing things they had never told a soul . . . I was beginning to see why Mama was usually so silent and tired, coming home from a Shamer's task. And some of the secrets she had seen were a lot worse than Nico's.

'Was it lonely?' asked Nico from his ledge. 'I mean – growing up with eyes like yours? Making friends cannot be easy, when they can't look you in the eye without blushing.'

'I don't have a lot of friends.' None whatsoever, in fact, but I didn't like to tell him that. 'But I have my family. Mama and Melli and particularly my older brother, Davin.' Then I suddenly started thinking about *his* older brother. *Do you yield?* And of Adela, whom I had seen in Nico's memory, alive and beautiful, and who now lay cold and dead and mutilated somewhere in the castle.

'Yes. Family.' He was silent for a while. 'Now that you know most of it, Dina – are you still not afraid of your monster?'

I had to take a minute to notice my feelings. Something had changed, of course. I had seen envy in him, and rage. Coldness. Callousness. And that hopeless, forbidden love for Adela. But not murder. Not blood and dead bodies. And he had been neither cold nor callous with me.

I did not answer him in so many words. I merely sat down next to him and took his hand.

'How brave you are,' he said. 'When I was your age I was afraid of nearly everything.' He was still breathing much too rapidly, and his hand was slick with sweat. 'Dina . . . If I fall asleep before Drakan comes back to get you, we . . . might not meet again. I want you to know that . . . that before you came, I thought that this last night would be a living hell. It . . . wasn't. Thanks to you.'

Suddenly, I felt cold all over. 'What do you mean – this last night. Why should it be the last? Mama knows you're innocent, and even Drakan is beginning to change his mind.'

There was a movement at the corner of his mouth, grimace or smile, it was hard to tell.

'Drakan has no illusions about my guilt.'

'But he said . . .'

'Drakan is fully convinced that I did it. But your mother has perhaps persuaded him that I was out of my head at the time. Not myself, so to speak. And for that reason he has given me his own kind of mercy.'

'Mercy? Nico, what are you talking about?'

'They say beheading is a painful death. And I have never been particularly brave. This . . . whatever it is that Drakan has put in his peace offering, it promises to be painless.'

'Nico!' Poison. He meant poison. That peace offering

– it was the peace of death that it would bring him. 'Sit up. You can't die now!'

'I may not have much choice in the matter.'

At least he had vomited up most of it, surely that had to help?

'Sit up straight, come on . . .' I pulled at his shoulder, trying to raise him, but he was about as co-operative as a rag doll. 'Come on!'

'Dina – please – leave me be . . .' His voice had become blurred and indistinct again. 'Leave me – in peace . . .'

'Yes, Dina. Leave him alone.'

I stiffened. It was Drakan's voice. He had returned, but without the lantern. I had not heard him approach.

Just exactly how long had he been standing in the dark, listening?

NINE

A Very Small Knife

In the silence, I could hear Nico breathe, too quickly, almost a pant, as if not enough air was getting into his lungs. Drakan stood just beyond the bars, a dark shadow with an invisible face. Could Nico be right about his so-called peace offering?

'What was in that bottle?' I asked.

'Wine,' said Drakan. 'He drinks too much and holds his liquor badly. Hasn't he told you that, now that you have become such friends?'

There was a sound from Nico, halfway between a gasp and a laugh. 'Oh, yes, cousin,' he said. 'She knows. She knows me inside out.'

Drakan was silent for a while, black and unmoving and almost hidden in the dark.

'So . . .' he finally said, in a thoughtful tone of voice. 'Her mother's daughter? Come here, little Shamer, and I'll let you out.'

'No.'

'No? What do you mean, no?'

'Not until you help him. Not until you tell us what

was in that bottle and what we can do to make him well.'

I could hear the key turning in the lock. 'Hasn't your mother taught you to obey your elders? Well, then, I suppose I'll just have to come and get you myself.'

'Help him first! He might . . . he might be dying!' Despair burnt hotly in my throat.

'Dina – please go . . .' said Nico in his raspy, winded way. 'Go with him.'

'No!' I clutched his hand and held it very tight. 'He'll help you. He has to. I *won't* let you die!'

The door opened, and Drakan entered the cell. He stood squarely in the middle of the moon stripe, but I still couldn't see his eyes. The hood of his cloak cast a shadow over most of his face. It wasn't the cloak he had been wearing that afternoon. This one was black, so black that it seemed to absorb the light around it.

'Come here, Dina,' he said, calmly and almost gently. 'Come to me.'

In the Dragon Pit that afternoon I had been so scared that I had not thought it possible that anyone could feel greater fear. I had been wrong. Right now, right here, I was more afraid of Drakan than I had ever been of the dragons. And wasn't there . . . wasn't there something of the dragon smell about him now, that harsh and rotten odour that had been so strong in the Pit?

I got up slowly, still holding Nico's hand.

'Why won't you help him?' I whispered. 'He is your cousin.'

Drakan moved a step closer, and now I was certain about the dragon smell.

'Cousin?' he sneered. 'Oh, that's really just a polite little lie. You see, when you are just a bastard son, you don't *really* belong to the family.' A fold of his cloak brushed my cheek, and I shuddered. What was that cloak *made* from? It felt cold and damp and raspy, like being licked by a cow.

'Cousin,' said Nico hoarsely. 'What was in that wine?'

Drakan went down on one knee beside me and put his arm around my shoulder. I tried to pull away, but his grip was very firm.

'Shall I tell you?' he said. 'Will that make your little friend here happy, do you think?' He rested his free hand on Nico's forehead for a moment. 'You really aren't feeling very well, are you? But I didn't poison your wine, dear cousin. On the contrary. I merely spiced it with dragon blood.'

'Dragon . . .' Nico panted even worse than before. 'Dragon blood?'

'Yes. Dragon blood is not a poison. It makes you swift and strong and helps you overcome numerous minor weaknesses. In small doses.' He patted Nico's cheek almost lovingly. 'Of course, you're not used to it. Perhaps it is too strong for you after all.'

Suddenly I knew what Drakan's cloak had been made from. It was a dragon hide. In the heather dales at home I had seen the adders shed their skin, leaving behind a strange empty ghost of themselves. Did dragons do the same thing? Or had he killed a dragon to get both skin and blood from it? And what did he mean by saying Nico wasn't used to it? Did he himself drink dragon's blood?

The cell door was open, only a few paces away. Somewhere, not very far away, was my mother. Somewhere even closer were people who did not smell like dragons and who did not drink dragon blood for breakfast. What was I waiting for?

I gave Nico's hand a small squeeze and then released it. With a sudden move, I twisted free of Drakan's grip and headed for the exit. I never reached it. Drakan lashed out with one foot, tripping me up, and I slammed full length into the cold stone floor. While I lay there, trying to get my breath back, he clanged the cell door shut and leaned against it, casually watching me.

'Where did you think you were going?' he asked. 'One minute I can barely drag you out of here, and the next you want to go charging off like a madwoman.'

Nico had pushed himself more or less upright on the ledge, but the effort was costly. His lungs were working like bellows, and the air whistled and wheezed in his throat.

'Leave – her – alone . . .' he gasped.

'Unfortunately, I can't,' Drakan said. 'I need her. But if you want to keep breathing a while yet, you had better lie down and keep still.'

'Need – her . . .' Nico managed. 'For – what?'

Still lying on the floor, I fumbled for my little knife, the one I had used to carve the soap with. The blade might be no longer than my finger, but it was still a knife, wasn't it? Whatever Drakan needed me for, I did not feel like being used by him. I got to my feet, clutching the knife, and tried to nail him to the wall with my eyes.

'*Let me go,*' I said in my best Shamer's voice. It only shook a very little.

He laughed, a harsh and humourless sound. 'They don't work on me, all your little Shamer tricks,' he said. 'You might as well go and stand in front of one of the dragons out there and try to make *it* feel ashamed. You might have more luck there.'

He hadn't locked the door, only closed it. I took a deep breath and started walking. I'd make him move, I thought. Actually, it seemed to surprise him to see me marching right into his reach. And when he finally made a grab for me, I plunged my knife into his hand. He yelped and let go of me, holding his hand up in front of him. Blood welled from a narrow cut in the palm, almost black in the moonlight.

'Devil brat,' he snarled. But he didn't move away from the door.

'Let me pass,' I said. 'Or I'll stab you again!'

This did not seem to frighten him very much. Actually, the shadow of a smile crossed his narrow lips.

'A knife,' he said thoughtfully. 'A very small knife, but still a knife.' He laughed again, and this time there was a note of triumph in it. 'This is so much better . . .' he said softly. 'I had meant to use my hands, but a knife is definitely better!'

I fervently wished that I had never shown him the knife. There was something hungry about the way he stared at me. Almost the sort of look our old cat used to give the mice it caught. This was before Beastie came to us, and the cat moved in at the smithy instead. And before I had even quite finished the thought, he moved. I'm not quite sure what he did. But a moment later he had his arm around my neck from behind and his other hand around the wrist of my knife hand. I think I screamed, or at least some sort of noise escaped me; I kicked at his leg and threw back my head, trying to butt his chin, but this was nothing like fighting Davin. The arm at my throat tightened, making it very hard to breathe, and his thumb dug into my wrist, deeply and painfully. I didn't want him to have the knife, and so I flung it away from me as hard as I could, which wasn't very hard. Drakan snarled something, but I couldn't make out the words. The pressure on my neck grew worse, and things started to go strangely red and blurry. I wanted to call for my mother, or Davin, or even Beastie, but they weren't there, and I had no air to shout with, and the red got darker and even more blurry and I was very much afraid that this was what dying felt like, this darkness, now . . . and then I could breathe again. I was crouched on all fours on the cell floor, taking one whooping gasp of air after the other, worse even than Nico. And right next to me lay Drakan, and he was breathing strangely too, a wet and gurgly sound that got weaker and weaker and finally stopped entirely.

I looked up. Nico was standing over us with my little knife in his hand, and both the blade and the hand were sticky with Drakan's blood.

'What happened?' I whispered, when I could speak again.

Nico just stood there, staring at the knife in his hand. 'I think I've killed him,' he finally said, in a peculiar thin voice, sounding no older than Melli. 'Now they'll have my head for sure.'

'He was trying to strangle me.'

'He said – he said . . .'

'Nico. Why did he try to strangle me?' I was shaking all over.

'They will think – you did it – he said . . .' Nico's breath was wheezier than ever. 'They will think – you killed – the Shamer's daughter . . .' He shuddered and shook himself, like a dog wanting to get rid of something in its fur. 'But he – was the one – that got killed . . .' He looked around wildly, confusedly. 'Out,' he gasped. 'We – have – to get – out – before they come . . .'

'Who?'

'Drakan's men. We must – get away . . .'

'Come on,' I said, getting to my feet. 'Let's go.'

There was a whistling sound from his chest for every step we took, and I made him put his arm over my shoulder though I really wasn't tall enough to give him much support. But a few steps down the passage, he suddenly came to a halt.

'The Pit,' he said. 'We need – the cloak . . .'

I didn't see why. I couldn't understand what he wanted that smelly, disgusting dragon hide for. But Nico would move no further without it, and so I finally made him lean against the wall while I went back to the cell.

Drakan still lay on the floor in the moonlight, wrapped in his black dragon hide. I didn't want to go any closer. I had seen dead animals – slaughtered pigs and lambs, and once the miller's mule which dropped dead one day in front of the cart and keeled over, harness and all. But I had never before seen a dead human being, and there was a difference.

'Nico . . .' I croaked, sounding like a frog. 'I'm not sure I can do this.'

'Let – me . . .' he said, but he could barely keep himself upright, and the thought of *two* dead people made me cold all over.

'No,' I said. 'Stay where you are. I'll manage.'

I took three quick paces into the cell, grabbed hold of the hem of the cloak and pulled. Drakan's body rolled on to its back, and the cloak came free. I held it out, stiff-armed, not wanting it to touch any part of my body. What a stench. But at least I could now get out of there, out of this jail and out through— and then I realized. If we were to get through the Dragon Pit, we needed Drakan's keys. Which meant that I would have to touch him.

How I wished that I could ask Nico to do it. Or that Davin was here, or Mama. Anyone at all. But there was only me. No one else, no way out. Just me. And so I bit my lower lip, crouched next to the corpse, closed my eyes and fumbled along his belt for the keyring.

And suddenly, something touched my leg.

I leaped to my feet and screamed my head off, and Nico came stumbling up the passage outside, with one hand on the wall.

'What – is it . . .'

I didn't answer. Petrified, I stared down at Drakan's hand, which had somehow closed itself around my ankle.

And while I stood there, staring, Drakan very very slowly turned his head and looked at me with his midnight blue eyes.

'Help me,' he whispered, almost soundlessly, but very clearly. On one side of his neck I could see the dark wound Nico had made. 'Give me the bottle.' His grip loosened, and the fingers opened like a spider giving up its prey. But his eyes still held me.

'The bottle . . .' I looked around. It lay just a pace or two away, but far, far out of Drakan's reach. Barely a mouthful or two remained of the contents. But what did he want with it? From where I stood, I could clearly hear Nico's tortured breathing. For a man wounded as badly as Drakan was, even those few mouthfuls might be enough to kill. And then I thought that that might be what he wanted. That it might hurt, and hurt badly, to lie there and be not quite dead. I gathered up the bottle and put it into his hand, and his fingers closed around it.

'Thank you,' he said and slowly brought the bottle to his lips. How much was left I really didn't know, but he sucked at it almost like a baby at the breast. And then he closed his eyes.

'Dina . . .' Nico called, as loudly as he could. 'We have — to go.'

I looked at Drakan one final time. Then I turned my back on him, not knowing whether he was still alive or not, took the dragon cloak and the keys, which I had dropped in my fright, and left him and the cell behind.

TEN

Lady Death

The guardroom at the end of the passage was empty. Drakan had probably sent them off on some errand – he would not have wanted witnesses for what he meant to happen in Nico's cell. It was lucky for us, however, as we would have had a hard time explaining why we were leaving a dead or dying Drakan back there. I poked my head cautiously around the corner, but the vault, too, was deserted.

'Stay here,' I told Nico. 'I'll get my mother.'

He nodded and slid down the wall, so that he could sit, leaning against it. There was only a single badly-trimmed lantern in the room, but even in that yellowish light he looked as pale as a corpse. He needed rest and treatment, not a scrambling escape through dragon pits and underground passages, I thought. We would have to pass through the Pit – but once my mother was with us, we had no need for further escape. She would be able to explain to people that Nico had used the knife on Drakan in self-defence, or rather, in defence of me. She was the Shamer. They would *have* to believe her. Or so

71

I told myself, as I sneaked through the vault and up the stairs to the room with the circle window. And somehow, I think I expected even the dragons to be in awe of my mother.

The door was not locked. I opened it and slipped inside. Moonlight streamed through the big round window where we had sat playing Even and Uneven – a very long time ago, it seemed to me. The drapes of the alcove were drawn, but I could hear the deep breathing of a sleeper inside.

'Mama,' I whispered, pulling back the drapes, 'Mama, wake up, you have to help—' and then I got no further. The woman in the bed was not my mother, but someone I had never seen before.

She opened her eyes. 'Have you done it?' she began, and only then seemed to see me properly. 'Who are *you*?' she asked, staring at me with expressionless eyes. There was a strange, sweet yet mouldy smell about her, the sort you get when you have forgotten to change the water in a flower vase and the stalks have begun to rot. Her cheeks were so sunken that her face was almost a skull. She looked like death, I thought. Lady Death. But the skinny fingers that suddenly reached out to grip my chin seemed strong enough. 'Let me see you . . .' She raised my chin so that the moonlight fell more clearly on me. 'The Shamer's daughter,' she whispered, looking away. 'She is your mother, isn't she?'

'Where is she?' I asked. 'Where is my mother?'

'Not here,' she said, fumbling for something under the pillows. 'But if you wait awhile, I shall show you—'

I never found out what she meant to show me. The smell had suddenly begun to make sense: a heavy perfume which could not quite overpower the stench of dragon blood. And when her hand emerged from under the pillows, it held a knife.

I threw myself to one side, so abruptly that I tripped and fell over backwards. A flurry of white down spiralled in the air between us; her first swing had sliced open the pillow, and she threw it aside in annoyance, trying to disentangle herself from the bed covers. I scuttled sideways, hit a table and overturned it, and thrust it in her direction. It hit her waist-high with enough force to knock her over. She tried to push it away with one skeletal hand, but she was unwilling to let go of the knife, and the table was too heavy for her to handle one-handed. My back met the wall, and I scrabbled to my feet and backed towards the open door. Tiny white feathers were whirling like snowflakes in the moonlight. She stabbed the knife into the tabletop from sheer fury, raised her head and howled, a shrill and wheezy scream like those the rats sometimes made when Beastie caught them.

For a moment, time seemed to stand still. Her grey-blue bedrobe had spread itself around her, so that it looked as if she was sitting on an ice floe. She had lost her white lace cap, and her long black hair had come tumbling down over her shoulders, reaching almost to her waist. Raven black it was, black as night, except for two chalky white locks framing her cheeks like wings. She stared at me with her dark eyes like craters in her yellow-white skull, and an icy cold seemed to suck the breath from my body, chilling the skin.

Stiff-legged I backed the last few steps on to the stairs, snatched at the door and slammed it shut between us. Leaning my full weight against it, I fumbled desperately for Drakan's keys. From the room came a loud crash – she had already managed to push the table aside. I forced a key into the lock, but it wasn't the right one. She tried to shove the door open, and although she looked to be hardly more than a skeleton, she was still stronger than I. The door gave under her weight and opened a crack before I managed to get it shut again. New key. Still not right. Third key . . . and the lock finally yielded, stiffly, creakingly, but it was the right key! I twisted with all my strength and heard the parts inside the lock turn and click. Again and again she screamed, stabbing at the door with her knife, but it was made from heavy oak timber, and there was no chance that she would be able to chop her way out.

For a while I just rested my back against the door, listening to her screams and the dull thunking of the knife blows. Oh, how I wanted to be somewhere else. To be home, right now. Home, where the kitchen was full of the scent of elderberries and roasted apples, with Melli begging for honey and Beastie scratching every now and then when a flea dared to bite him. Home in my own bed, home with Davin, home with Mama. Home, where no one was trying to strangle me, stab me or eat me. A drawn-out sniffle tore at my chest, and tears were making my eyes sting and were starting to spill and trickle down my cheeks. I was about ready to give in. I could easily have crouched there for ever, waiting for someone to come and rescue me. But Nico did not have that kind of time. And wherever Mama was, it obviously wasn't here. I sniffed once more and wiped my face with my sleeve. Then I ran down the stairs, through the vault, and into the guardroom.

Nico was still squatting where I had left him, but when he saw me, he struggled to his feet.

'Dina . . .' Even such a short rest had eased his breathing somewhat. 'You look like . . . What happened?'

'Mama wasn't there,' I croaked, the tears I was holding back threatening to rob me of what voice I had. 'There was a . . . a Lady Death. She tried to stab me with a knife!'

He put his hand on my shoulder, and suddenly I couldn't help myself; I just had to wrap my arms around him and hide my face against his shoulder. He stroked my hair and rested his hand against my cheek.

'You're chilled. But Dina – I don't think – ghosts really exist. Not here, at any rate.'

'She was no ghost! She was a human being, a real live human being, only . . .' I struggled to explain to him how Lady Death had looked.

'Oh,' he said. 'You mean Dama Lizea. My aunt. Drakan's mother – she has been ill – that's why she – looks so thin.'

I wiped the tears off my face with the inside of my wrist. Drakan's mother! That explained why she had attacked me – except . . . how could she know that her son was dead? Or *might* be dead.

'But Dina – are you sure – about the knife? You don't think – you might be mistaken? That it was – something else?'

I shook my head. 'It *was* a knife.' I could still see it in my mind, pale and shiny in the moonlight, nearly as long as my lower arm. 'She cut open a pillow by mistake, there were feathers all over the place.'

'All right, but what did you do? Where is she now?'

'I locked her in the room.'

'You . . .' He put his hands on my shoulders and held me at arm's length, studying me. 'You – locked her in. Well, that's one way – of solving the problem.' He suddenly started to laugh, still a bit wheezy, but definitely a laugh. 'Do you know – I think I'll just sit down for a while – If I wait – a couple of hours – you'll no doubt – have conquered – the whole castle – single-handed.'

Oh no. No way was he going to get away with that!

'You're coming with me!' I said angrily. 'I am *not* walking past those dragons on my own!'

He became serious again immediately. 'Dina. It was a *joke* – I would never desert you like that.' He squeezed my shoulder gently. 'But I suppose – we had better see – what we can do about – those dragons.'

'Can't we wait until morning?'

'No.' He shook his head emphatically. 'If we are to get away unseen – we must make use – of the darkness.'

I closed my eyes for a moment, trying to blink back the tears.

'If that's the way it has to be,' I said as calmly as I could, 'then we might as well get it over with.'

He nodded. 'We'd better. Time is short.'

And so we took the dragon hide cloak and the lantern from the guardroom and made for the Pit.

ELEVEN

Draco Draco

The Dragon Pit was cold. The chill struck at us through the bars of the gate, even before we entered. Parts of the Pit were made up out of old cellar passages like those we came from, but once, a very long time ago, the vaults and the buildings on top of them had collapsed, so that the ruins now were open to the icy, black sky. Moss and tiny toadstools grew from cracks and furrows in the rubble and rotting old timber. Other than that, the dragons were the only live things in the Pit.

I wanted to bring the lantern, but Nico said we would be better off without it. What the light falls on, you see clearly enough, he said. But you become blind to everything that moves in the darkness. If we stumbled through the ruins beautifully lit by our own lantern and unable to see anything outside its narrow circle of light, the dragons would have a field day. So we stood for a while by the gate, trying to accustom our eyes to the dim moonlight instead.

I could see no dragons at the moment.

'Do they sleep at night?' I whispered.

'I don't know,' Nico answered, also in a whisper. 'We had better not count on it.'

He had got hold of Drakan's spear and had draped the stinking cloak around his shoulders. When I complained about it, he just shrugged. 'If you smell like a dragon – perhaps they will think you *are* a dragon,' he said.

Suddenly he stiffened. 'There,' he mumbled, pointing. At first I still couldn't see any dragons. Then I caught sight of a slithery movement in the shadows beneath a half-crumbled vault. They lay in a huddle, neck over neck, tail over tail, looking like giant snakes because we couldn't see their legs. Perhaps they were helping each other keep warm. Mama once told me that adders and lizards couldn't heat their own bodies, and that this was why they often lay on rocks during the daytime, soaking up the heat of the sun. On the other hand, they could get very cold without dying from it, like a hot-blooded creature would. I must never think an adder was dead, she had said, no matter how still and cold it seemed.

The night was very cold. Hoar-frost lay like a white crust over much of the rubble in the Pit. Perhaps, like the adders, the dragons then would have to be very still?

'Draco Draco,' whispered Nico. 'Here we come.' He unlocked the final gate.

'Why do you say that?'

'What?'

'That . . . that dracodraco thing.'

'Oh . . . that's their proper name. In Latin.'

I stared at the worm pile under the vault. I didn't care what they were called – in Latin or otherwise. 'How nice. Now I can be polite to them while they're eating me.'

I swear he smiled, the idiot. How could he smile *now*?

'Think of them as overgrown lizards,' he said, pushing open the gate.

I wanted most of all to rush across the Pit, running as fast as I could. But Nico had told me not to. The stones were damp and slippery with frost, and rubble and old timbers were just waiting to trip you up. If one of us twisted an ankle and was no longer able to walk, the dragons would make an easy meal of us. So we did not run. We walked. I stayed very close to Nico and his spear and kept my eyes glued to the dragons, and so I nearly tripped myself up after all, stumbling over a rotting beam sticking out of the rubble. Nico grabbed my elbow and kept me from falling. My heart was pounding so loudly that I thought the sound would rouse the dragons. They weren't totally still, over there in the huddle. At first the clutch was so tightly coiled that it was hard to tell where one dragon left off and another began. But gradually, one monster started to emerge from the tangle.

'Nico!' I whispered frantically.

'I've seen it,' he said, clutching his spear more tightly. 'Keep walking.'

That was all very well for him to say. My legs felt stiff and strange, my whole body felt strange, rushing and pounding and buzzing with fear. If that dragon took one more step . . .

And it did. One step, two steps, a slow, writhing waddle, its head lowered, no more than a foot or so off the ground . . . onwards it came, and as it slipped from the shadows and into the moonlight, the scales gleamed like mother-of-pearl, and the long, long body curved like a winding river, huge and glittery. I could see its jaws and the split tongue that kept flickering out, then in, then out again, as if it was tasting the air.

'Move!' Nico hissed, and I only then realized that I had come to a complete halt. The only thing I wanted to do was run, run, run, and never stop, and yet here I was, feet stuck to the ground as if they had weights on them.

Almost the worst of it was the *slowness*. I couldn't help myself – I just had to stare at it, watching it flow forward inch by inch like a wave of thick mud. I could see its pale yellow eyes clearly now. Slowly it raised its head, swaying from side to side. Slowly it opened its jaws, bluish purple and full of needle-sharp fangs . . .

If not for Nico, I might have stood there gaping at the eyes and jaws and teeth of the dragon until it finally ate me. But he grabbed my arm and forced me onward, even though my legs seemed not to want to follow.

'Don't look at it so,' he said. 'Watch the gate instead. Make sure we stay on course – I'll keep an eye on the beast.'

I forced my eyes away from the dragon and looked towards the gate instead. And that was when I knew we were going to die.

In front of the gate, blocking our way, a dragon lay coiled. It was taller, wider and longer than any of the others. It seemed to take up all the space between us and the gate. Its yellow eyes stared at me from above, and it was close enough for me to see a milky-white drop of venom at the end of each fang.

I wet myself.

It would have been nice to be able to say that I faced the dragon calmly and bravely. But I didn't. Instead, a warm and wet trickle of pee shot down one leg. A thin, birdlike sound emerged from my throat – not quite a scream, I had no air to scream with. The dragon drew back its head, and I knew it was going to strike. I had no thoughts. I didn't think of Nico at all, or of Mama. My head was just a thin shell around a big, empty fog of grey terror. It would soon be over, and I wouldn't even fight it. No more than the dead calf had done.

Something came flying through the air, and suddenly the yellow eyes were gone. A dark shroud enfolded the dragon's head – the dragon hide cloak, I now saw. Then a hard shove made me fall to one side, and Nico was rushing the blindfolded dragon, spear in hand. The dragon flung up its head, trying to get rid of whatever was blinding it, but the cloak clung to it like some huge black bat. And then Nico thrust his spear into its throat, just below the jaw. A shower of black blood washed over him, and he lost his grip on the spear. But his aim had been good. The dragon fell forwards, still blinded by the cloak, and although it tried to bat at the spear with its long claws, I could see that it was dying. Scrambling and writhing, it tumbled on to its back, and the blood was still gushing from its throat, making the ground around it muddy and dark.

Had the big dragon been the only one in the Pit, we would have escaped from there without a scratch. Nico stood, staring down at the dying monster, a funny expression on his face. Killing a dragon probably wasn't an everyday experience for him. And I got to my feet again and felt like a louse, a very insignificant little louse, because he had been so strong and clever and brave, while I had just stood there, wetting myself. And both of us were being stupid, for there was no time to think of dragon killing *or* of lice.

Claws clicked on the rocks behind us. That was all I had time to hear before the second dragon struck. Nico desperately threw himself to one side, rolling on the ground, and nearly made it to his feet again – but then the tail of the dying dragon slammed into him, knocking him to the ground and pinning him there. It might as well have been a tree trunk – he had no chance of getting out from under it in time; the other dragon was already preparing its second strike.

It's one thing to be a louse when you are about to be eaten. It is quite another to stand by and watch while a dragon eats someone else, someone you happen to like and care about. I had no spear and no cloak. But there were rocks aplenty. I grabbed a brick and hefted it. Davin and I used to throw stones at the rats in the stable. And a dragon is much easier to hit. The brick sailed through the air just the way I wanted it to, and hit the monster on the nose, bang on target.

It jerked and shook its head. I grabbed another rock, took aim and fired. Slowly it turned its attention from Nico to me. And that was it, of course. It was *slow*. As long as I didn't stand there like some bleating lamb in a wolf trap, I could easily stay out of its reach. I danced sideways, picking up another rock. Yelling and screaming and pelting it with stones, I circled the dragon until it nearly got itself in a knot, trying to keep an eye on me.

'Hey there, dragon!' I yelled. 'Stupid dragon! Draco-draco-draco . . .' All the while I was watching out of the corner of my eye as Nico battled with the dragon tail and gradually managed to pull himself free of it. He climbed over the body of the dying dragon and wrested the spear from its throat.

'Quick, Dina! Get behind the dead one!'

Dead it wasn't, not quite. But I got the point. Its body would provide us with some cover while we got the gate open. And hanging about would be a really bad idea. The huddle under the vault had completely uncoiled itself now and four more dragons were coming. I threw my last rock and dived for cover.

I made it, too – more or less. I raced across rocky ground, broken beams, and rubble without putting a foot wrong, leaping across the long outstretched dragon neck to join Nico, who stood, spear at the ready, keeping the other dragon at bay. And as I stood there, fumbling for the key, within *reach* of the gate, there, just a few feet away . . . while I stood there, pushing the key into the lock, the dying dragon raised its head one last time, dislodging the cloak so that it was finally able to see again. I didn't have time to scream. It hissed once and closed its jaws around my left arm.

Its fangs went through cloth and skin and muscle, all the way to the bone. It had no strength left to shake me, as Beastie did with the rats he caught. I could see the scales darkening, turning black as life left it. Its head sank to the ground again, and I had to follow, until I was kneeling by its side, my arm still trapped in its jaws. Its one yellow eye stared at me, and I knew it would never let go, not even in death. In a way it didn't hurt as much as you would think – my arm went numb almost right away – but I couldn't move an inch.

'Nico . . .' I whispered, not having the strength to shout. The darkness had somehow become darker, and all I could really see was the dragon's yellow eye. But I could hear Nico's shocked voice.

'Dina! *No* . . .'

Then the dragon's grip suddenly loosened. Nico had pushed the spear between its teeth and forced its jaws apart. My arm slipped out and hung from my shoulder like a lump of meat. Dimly I heard the sound of the key in the lock. But what about the other dragon – *all* the other dragons? Why weren't they attacking?

'Try to get up. Dina, come *on*, you can't give in now . . .'

Nico hauled on my healthy arm, dragging me to my feet. Uncertainly, half-blind, I stumbled the last few steps through the gate, then dropped to my knees again, unable to keep my balance once I had heard the gate clang shut and knew we were safe. And through the bars of the gate I saw why the other dragons hadn't attacked us. They were too busy. Hungrily, they had already begun to tear apart the body of their dying pitmate.

TWELVE

Master Maunus

Blue stripes were shimmering in front of my eyes. Somewhere, very far away, Rikert Smith had placed my arm on his anvil and was busily pounding away at it, as though he was making ploughshare. My head hurt madly, and the air, thick with oily lamp smoke and other fumes, was not making it any better. My eyelashes were gummed together, making it terribly hard to open my eyes properly. When I finally succeeded, I found that it was still dark, and that whatever room I was in was lit only by two dim candles.

'Will it be morning soon?' I whispered hoarsely. Surely it *had* to be near dawn. No night could be this long.

'The morning has been and gone,' said a strange voice somewhere in the darkness. 'It's night-time again.'

I felt so miserable. I had been longing for an end to the darkness, so that I would be able to breathe in sunshine and daylight and fresh, free air. And here he was, telling me I had missed it, and that there was yet another endless night to get through. Tears began to trickle from the corners of my eyes, and because I was lying down, they did not run down my cheeks, but sideways, towards my ears.

'Hush, now,' said the voice. 'Be easy. Sleep. When you wake up, the sun will be shining.'

I closed my eyes, praying he was right. But as I slept, my mind filled with dragon dreams and nightmares of Nico dragging me down endless corridors, on and on, and I was so tired, everything hurt, but the arm most of all, thudding, thudding, thudding.

But the voice turned out to be right after all. When I woke up again, a long, narrow square of sunlight fell across the blue-striped covers of my bed. My arm was still throbbing, but not as violently. And Nico was sitting next to my bed, watching me with frightened eyes.

'Are you awake?' he asked. 'How are you?'

'All right,' I said, or tried to say. It came out like a croak. 'Where are we?'

'With Master Maunus.'

'Who is Master Maunus?'

'I am,' said the voice I had heard in the night. It belonged to a tall man – a very tall man, perhaps the biggest I had ever seen – with fiery red hair and a great red bush of a moustache. There was a dusting of crumbs on the moustache. He was wearing a worn, green velvet suit, and a scent of iodine and alcohol hung around him.

'Are you a doctor?' I asked; I knew that smell from my mother.

He shook his head. 'An alchemist.'

If my eyelashes had not still been gummed up, my eyes would have widened. 'A goldmaker?'

He shook his head again, this time with a show of annoyance.

'A scientist. Goldmaking is for tricksters and ignorant amateurs; it cannot be done. A true alchemist works with the elements and their chemistry in a sober and scientific manner. Something which I was never able to impress on the simple boy at present trying to dismantle your pillowcase.'

Nico snorted, but let go of the thread he had been picking at.

'The world contains nothing so wonderful, amazing and fantastic that Master Maunus is not able to render it deadly dry and boring,' he said. 'I know. He was my tutor for nine years.'

Master Maunus frowned so hard that his bushy red eyebrows nearly met in the middle. 'An ill-fated time,' he said. 'But your stupidities then were as nothing to the sublime idiocy you are capable of these days. Why will you not see that—'

'Maunus,' Nico interrupted. 'Not now...' He waved a hand in my direction, a heavy and tired motion.

'No, you are right,' Maunus said. 'Not now. It is time for the young lady's breakfast.' He disappeared behind a heavy, dark blue curtain that shielded the entrance to the cubby-hole I was in. I scrutinized Nico a bit more carefully and was happy to see that he was no longer gasping for breath. He looked tired and pale, and his battered face had become mottled yellow and black down one side, but he no longer looked like a dying man.

'Are *you* all right?' I asked.

'Well enough,' he said. 'Battling a dragon appeared to be just what it took to purge the last of the poison from my body. The effect was not lethal – as you can see.'

'But Nico – what are we doing here? Where is my mother?'

He looked away. 'Everything is a bit complicated at the moment. They say Drakan is lying in his mother's chambers, hovering between life and death after what they call my attempt on his life. His men and the other guards are all searching for me. They think I have carried you off and am holding you captive somewhere.'

'Captive?'

'So they say.'

'And Mama? Where is she?'

'We don't know. None of the people Master Maunus has dared to ask have seen her these past two days.'

Tears again started to trickle towards my ears. I couldn't seem to help myself. Everything was just so frightening and confusing, and my arm hurt so. And Mama. If I had to worry that something might have happened to Mama . . .

'Dina . . . please. Please don't cry. We'll figure something out. It'll be fine!'

'If something has happened to my mother . . .' I took a deep breath and tried to stop crying, but it wasn't easy.

'No one would dare to hurt a Shamer. We'll find her. Just you wait and see.'

The curtain was drawn aside, and Master Maunus reappeared.

'Right now it is enough that the young lady concentrate on her soup,' he said. 'Out you go, Young Master Dunce. Get some sleep. I've made you up a bed of sorts in the wood bin in the laboratory. It may be a bit on the short side, but none of the castle staff like to poke around in the workshop, and you can close the lid in seconds if we have visitors.'

Nico made no objections. He was so tired that he was swaying as he stood up.

'It'll be fine, Dina,' he repeated.

'Yes,' I said. 'Sleep well.'

He nodded vaguely and made uncertainly for the exit. Master Maunus held the curtain to let him pass, then let it fall.

'Is he going to be . . . Master Maunus, will he be all right?'

The red-haired man nodded. 'He needs the rest. He has slept very little since he brought you here, and I imagine even less the night before that. He has had to bear more than is good for any man. But here. Can you hold the bowl yourself?'

As it turned out, I couldn't. The dragon-bitten arm would not work at all. Master Maunus had to support the tray for me, but at least I was able to lift the spoon myself with my good hand. The soup was full of veal, carrots, potatoes and dill. It tasted perfectly wonderful, and once I had emptied the bowl, I felt like a new person. Not surprising, really. When I thought about it, I realized that this was my first meal since the lunch I had eaten two days ago at Cherry Tree Cottage.

Master Maunus grinned when he saw how quickly the soup was disappearing.

'Feeling better now?' he said, when the bowl was empty.

'Yes. Much better.'

'If you have to pee, use the chamber pot here,' he said and showed me how to open the little compartment it was kept in. 'We can't have you walking the corridors right now, with the whole castle guard looking for you.'

'But Master Maunus – if they are looking for Nico and me, and you were his tutor for such a long time, won't they come to you?'

'Not straight away,' he said, a strangely saddened expression on his face. 'Everyone knows that young Nicodemus and I had a furious argument two years ago and have not spoken since.'

'For two years? Over an argument?' I could hear the disbelief in my own voice. Davin and I fought all the time. If we were to stop talking every time we had an argument, we would *never* talk.

Master Maunus made an uneasy, growling sound. 'Maybe it was a bit more than an argument. As I recall, I brained him with a brass alembic. But not even that seemed to knock a smidgen of sense into his head.' He still looked angry at the thought.

'But if you and he are not on speaking terms – why did he come to you for help?'

Master Maunus placed the tray on the small table next to the bed.

'Because he knew I would not refuse him,' he said, not looking at me.

I stared at him. I would never understand these people. Quarrelling, yes, that I could understand. Not speaking for two years . . . that was harder to imagine, but if one was furious enough, then yes, perhaps. Not speaking for two years, yet *knowing* that the other person would help you no matter what you had been accused of – that went beyond my comprehension.

Master Maunus seemed to have been reading my thoughts.

'We are both incredibly stubborn,' he muttered. 'He is young and stupid and stubborn, and I am ageing and a bit wiser but just as stubborn. But for many years I was more of a father to him than the Castellan ever was. They were fire and ice, those two. Did not understand each other at all.'

One of Nico's memory pictures suddenly rose in my mind: his father beating him over and over again, shouting at him that 'a man is nothing without his sword'. I could well understand why Nico had needed someone to care for him.

'It was probably stupid of you to hit him,' I said, without thinking about how rude that might sound. But he simply nodded.

'Very stupid. He got enough of that from the Castellan. I shouldn't have . . . but the boy would not *listen*. Nothing did any good. It was as if he had made up his mind to throw everything away, everything he had and was, everything he might have become. And so . . . it happened. Two years. But still – still, it was to me he came when he needed help. He knew that much, at least.' He seemed to stand straighter at the thought.

'And how long will it be before the castle guards know it too?' I asked.

'They will come here sooner or later. If nothing else, they will make a thorough search of the entire castle, once they have been to all the more obvious places without finding him. But I do have a plan.' He raised one side of the mattress and moved some planks. 'Look,' he said. 'There is a compartment down here that I use when I work with fine metals and have a need to stow them safely and secretly. It might be big enough for a girl your size.'

It was not a wide space, but I would be able to fit in there, though I would probably not be any more comfortable than Nico in his wood bin. Master Maunus closed the compartment again and let the mattress settle in its place.

'And now we had better check that arm of yours.'

It was not a pretty sight. There were six deep triangular tears between the elbow and the wrist where the dragon had sunk its fangs, and the entire lower arm was swollen and blue-black. But Master Maunus seemed to be just as interested in what the arm looked like above the elbow.

'No sign of blood poisoning,' he said with some satisfaction. 'Can you move your fingers?'

I tried. At first they would not obey me at all. Then three of them began to show signs of life. But the little finger and the finger next to it remained stubbornly unmoving. Master Maunus made another growling sound at the back of his throat.

'Perhaps when the swelling goes down and the wounds heal. Keep trying,' he said. 'Damn beasts. I suppose they are biologically quite interesting, but I fail to see the need to keep so many of them.'

'Where do they come from?'

'They were a part of Dama Lizea's dowry. Or some of them were. They have bred since, and a few of them have grown to quite improbable sizes. But of course, you know that.'

'Oh yes,' I muttered darkly, eyeing my poor arm. 'Isn't that a peculiar thing to have for a dowry?'

He sighed. 'Dama Lizea's father is a peculiar man. And it happened to be a rather peculiar wedding, at that. But many lords would actually pay a pretty sum for those monsters.'

'But why?'

'Something to do with respect. If a man owns something rare and terrible – would you not respect him?'

'I'm not sure. Be afraid of him, perhaps.'

'There you are. To some lords, that is the same as respect.'

We were left alone at Master Máunus's for another full day. But that night, just as I had fallen asleep in the alcove under the blue-striped covers, my host came to shake me awake, gently but hurriedly.

'Shh . . .' he whispered. 'Quick. Into the compartment. Guards coming.'

My heart was knocking against my ribs as I rolled out

of bed so that Master Maunus could lift up the mattress and push aside the boards. Everything seemed unreal and nightmarish, perhaps because I had just been shaken out of a dream. The sound of booted heels in the corridor was certainly real enough. Master Maunus ripped the last of the boards up so quickly that we later found that his hands were full of splinters from the rough, unsanded wood.

'Get down there.'

I squeezed into the small compartment, and the boards went back in any old how, just as someone tried to open the door to the chambers.

'Make no sound, no matter what happens!' Maunus whispered, fitting the mattress back in place, so that my cramped little space became totally dark. There was a crash and more booted footsteps, and then I felt the bedboards move and creak, as Master Maunus took my former place in the rumpled bed.

'What is the meaning of this?' he roared angrily. 'What do you mean by . . . You! Hob Turnkey! Why have you smashed my door – and at this hour of the night!'

'I have my orders,' barked a voice, Hob the Turnkey's, I supposed. Then the voice gentled somewhat. 'And it's not exactly the middle of the night, Master.'

There was a lot of noise from cupboards and chest lids being wrenched open and a crash of broken glass. A sour and frightened taste was in my mouth. The wood bin – it was such an obvious hiding place, meant only to deceive the most casual search. And this search did not sound casual. Surely they must find him any minute now?

'Watch out, man!' cried Master Maunus at the sound of yet more glass breaking. 'Some of that stuff is dangerous! Stay away from that cabinet, I'll open it myself . . .' Another crash, and then a bellow from the alchemist, loud enough to shiver the window panes: '*Noooo!* Hold your breath! Out, everybody, *out*, as you value your lives!'

'Wait!' shouted Hob Turnkey, but judging from the pounding of running feet, his order had little effect. None of his men wanted to stay and breathe in one of the alchemist's dangerous substances. I grew scared too, or more so, for there really was a sharp and terrible smell that reached me even through the mattress, a sharpness that made the eyes water and the throat and nose burn. But Master Maunus had told me to stay put *no matter what*, and so I did.

A door slammed. Then there was a silence in Master Maunus's chambers, though I could hear angry and excited voices further off and what sounded like a struggle. Were they hurting Master Maunus? I had seen the bruises on Nico's face and upper body, and I knew the guards did not always deal gently with the people in their charge.

Then there was a crash as the door flew back on its hinges, and the thud of a body hitting the wall.

'That's enough, old man! I'm tired of your tricks. *Where is he?*'

This time, it wasn't Hob Turnkey.

This time, it was Drakan himself.

THIRTEEN

The Order of the Dragon

Had the compartment always been this small? It felt as if I didn't even have room to breathe, and my head filled with stories of people being buried alive. Mind you, I had never heard of anyone being buried alive inside a bed, but there is a first time for everything. And if something happened to Master Maunus – would I even be able to push back the bedboards and the mattress on my own, with only one good arm?

Out there in the rooms they were quarrelling loudly. But then, they had all the air they could breathe. Drakan did not sound as if he was hovering between life and death. As a matter of fact, he seemed extraordinarily alive – and extraordinarily furious.

'I know he's here,' he snarled, and there was another reverberating thud. Perhaps he was shoving Master Maunus against the wall. 'Why else the circus act? There are no lethal gases here, just a bit of ammonia. Fools! To run like a pack of frightened girls from something found in any pigsty! Continue the search!'

I bit my lip. Master Maunus's diversion had not

succeeded – he had only made them all the more suspicious. Any minute now they would open the wood bin. And that would be that.

'Why would I shelter a murderer? We were enemies *before* he committed his foul deed. Why would we suddenly become friends now?'

Drakan gave a bitter laugh. 'You were never enemies, old man. He was always your favourite. Even when you quarrelled. Oh yes. He would know to come here for help.'

A sheepish guard made his report. 'Mesire, he really isn't here. We've searched everywhere.'

How could that be true? Could they possibly have overlooked the wood bin? Surely they weren't that stupid.

'He *must* be here. Why else the ammonia stunt?'

'For a moment I thought it was chlorine,' Master Maunus growled. 'An honest and natural mistake, that's all.'

'A mistake?' Drakan snorted. 'The day you mistake ammonia for chlorine is the day you have stopped breathing. But watch out, old man. That time may come before you know it. A new Order is being born. And we will not deal gently with traitors!'

More booted feet. More orders. Then silence. I couldn't believe my own ears. They had left without discovering us!

It was quite a while before Maunus dared let me out of my hiding place, and even then he laid a careful finger on his lip and gestured for me to be silent. I looked aghast at the wreckage of his well-ordered home and workshop. What a sight! Broken glass everywhere. The blue curtain was torn to shreds, and all the cabinet doors in the workshop had been wrenched off their hinges. Some of the damage was quite clearly vengeance for the fruitless search. Why, for instance, had they smashed Master Maunus's pretty blue tobacco jar? Had they imagined Nico to be hiding in that?

Nico stood hunched and pale by the window, surveying the ruins.

'I'm sorry about this,' he said, gesturing at the mess. 'All your work, all your things . . .'

'Things. That's all they are,' said Master Maunus, gently shaking bits of broken glass from some papers he had picked up off the floor. 'I was lucky they did not burn all my formulas. Now, *that* would have been a disaster.'

'We can't stay here,' Nico quietly pointed out. 'We can't let you risk this again – or something even worse.'

'You can't walk out of that door either.' Maunus smoothed the papers lovingly, as though stroking a child's cheek. 'I would be much surprised if Drakan has not put some sort of a spy or guard in the corridor or on the stairs. I certainly would in his place. And he is not a stupid man.'

'It's a wonder that he's not a dead one. I was so sure I had killed him. And when he asked for the bottle of dragon blood, I thought it was to end the pain.'

'So did I,' I said. 'But he seems more alive than ever!'

'Actually, that's not so surprising if he is drinking dragon blood,' Master Maunus announced, in a tone that suggested that this was something every dimwit should know.

'What do you mean?'

'The blood of Draco Draco contains a very effective stimulant. Otherwise they would kill each other off every time they got into a fight over a bit of meat or a sunny spot. Because of the venom.'

I remembered the milky-white drops of venom glittering on the dragon's fangs and shuddered. 'Do you mean that . . . that they aren't hurt by the venom of other dragons because of this thing in their blood?'

'Yes. The venom has a deadening and partially paralysing effect. It isn't lethal in itself – or you would not still be with us, young lady. It is merely used to keep the prey helpless and immobile while the dragon prepares to swallow it.'

I shuddered again. It had come close to being a strongly personal experience, that bit about being paralysed and swallowed. 'So when Drakan drinks the blood . . .'

'The stimulant in the blood is meant to act as an antidote to the venom. So when Drakan drinks the blood without having been affected by the venom, he becomes as you saw him, or heard him, to be precise; manic, excitable and almost too alive. In the short term it may have saved him from dying of systemic shock and brought him back on his feet faster than seems humanly possible. In the long run, I doubt that it is a very healthy habit.'

I had more or less stopped listening. I had caught sight of the wood bin – or rather, what was left of it: it was now fit only for kindling.

'Nico . . . Where were you? Why didn't they find you?'

He smiled secretively. 'Oh, I was out getting myself a bit of fresh air.'

'*Out?* How?' He couldn't possibly have made it through the door, and the window – the window faced a wonderful view and a dizzying, vertical drop off the edge of Dun Rock.

'Have a look.' He carefully eased the window open and showed me how he had done his disappearing act. Just below the window was an iron boss in the shape of a rusty cross, and he had managed to force a rope between the top arm of the cross and the brick wall. From the rope he had formed a sort of sling with a loop for each leg.

'I was out here, swinging peacefully, while those beasts tore up Master Maunus's rooms.'

I leaned out, taking in the view and the long, long drop. If I had been the one swinging, there would have been nothing peaceful about it. I would have been completely terrified.

'I thought you said you weren't particularly brave.'

He met my gaze with complete honesty and openness for a moment. 'It's wonderful how brave you suddenly become when you are trying to avoid getting your head chopped off.' Then he sighed and broke off the brief eye contact. 'This doesn't get us any further. We simply can't stay here, and yet Master Maunus is right about the guard on the door.'

I was tired, and my arm hurt. I had done nothing except lie in a dark hole shaking with fear, but if I am anything to go by, a dose of terror can drain your strength more than a full day's work at harvest time.

'Is it safe to go to sleep, even?' I asked. 'What if they come back in the middle of the night?'

'I'll keep watch for the first part of the night,' Master Maunus volunteered. 'I'm staying up anyway to try to clear some of this mess away. Then Nicodemus can watch for the remaining hours. But if you can stand it, Dina, it would be better for you to sleep actually in the compartment, so that we only have to fling down the boards and the mattress. We nearly didn't make it this time.'

And so we put some extra pillows down to make it a bit more comfortable, and I tried to think of it as a snug little nest, rather than, for instance, an open coffin. It may even have worked. Or else I was simply so tired that I could have slept anywhere.

In the middle of the night I came awake abruptly, roused by what sounded like a fight and somebody screaming *No! No! No!* I was convinced that Drakan's men had found us, but it turned out to be Nico, lying on the mattress next to the bed, crying out and flailing his arms about, while Master Maunus was trying to wake him up and calm him down. Finally Nico came to his senses and stopped screaming.

'It's just a nightmare, Nico . . .' said the big alchemist, holding him like a child. 'Hush, boy, hush, it's all right.'

It was the first time I ever heard Master Maunus calling him anything except Nicodemus or Young Master Dunce.

'I know, I know. I'm awake now. But they were all lying there, and there was blood all over and – Master, it's true. It's real. That's the way it was. Adela and Bian. My *father*.'

'Yes. That's the way it was. And it's an evil thing. But it was not your fault.'

'I don't even know that!'

'Yes, you do. And if you have any doubts, ask me. Or your little friend here. Or her mother. We all know you didn't do it. And if you cannot sleep, at least you must rest a little.'

'Master . . . May we have a lamp in here? So that I can see where I am?'

'Yes,' said Master Maunus. 'We can do that.'

The rest of the night was quite peaceful. But in the middle of breakfast, Nico and I had to rush to our hiding places. I lay in the compartment with the mugs and dishes resting on my chest, so that it would not be obvious that more than one person had been at the table. Nico hung in his sling out there in the bright morning sunshine, hoping that none of the fishermen or mussel gatherers down there on the mud flats would look up and find it peculiar that a young man spent such a long time 'repairing' the masonry above their heads.

This time, however, it was neither Drakan nor his guards.

'Have you seen it?' asked a voice the minute Master Maunus opened his door. 'Have you seen it? The whole town is plastered with them. He must have had the scribes working all night.'

'Goodmorrow, Master Chamberlain. Have I seen what?'

'This!'

There was a momentary silence while Master Maunus looked at whatever it was that had so outraged the Chamberlain.

'I see,' he then said, quite curtly. 'It had to come, I suppose. After what Drakan said yesterday.'

'Drakan? He was here?'

'Who else? Or did you think I had suddenly taken a violent dislike to my own furniture?'

It seemed that the Chamberlain only now took proper notice of his surroundings.

'Good God! What a mess!'

'Drakan appears to have been labouring under the misapprehension that I was hiding Mesire Nicodemus among my test tubes.'

'And you aren't? I mean, not among the test tubes, of course, but somewhere else? Good Master Maunus, do you know where the young lord may be found?'

'No,' replied the alchemist casually. 'Why?'

'Because we . . . because I think the young lord should know that there are certain people who believed in his innocence even before this.' There was a rustling of paper. 'That belief has now become certitude!'

'Softly, my good Chamberlain, softly. These are beliefs that should not be spoken in such ringing tones.'

The Chamberlain lowered his voice immediately. 'You are right, good friend. Yet spoken they must be!'

'Was there anyone in the corridors or on the stairs when you came up?'

'No . . . well, there was the fellow washing them — the stairs, that is.'

'Thank you, Master Chamberlain. Thank you for coming, and thank you for your good words. But we must tread softly yet awhile. Be careful, and speak only to those you are certain of.'

'I shall be most cautious. Farewell, Goldmaster.'

'You know I hate that preposterous title!'

'Yes — that is why I use it.'

Master Maunus snorted. 'Farewell then, Chamberlain.'

It felt like an eternity before Master Maunus finally came to remove the mattress and set me free to satisfy my curiosity. In the workshop Nico was standing, holding a scroll of rough, yellow paper in his hand. I began to read over his shoulder.

Proclamation

it said. And then:

It is hereby made known to every good citizen of Dunark:

- that Nicodemus Ravens, youngest son of Lord Ebnezer Ravens of Dunark, has this day been found guilty of patricide and of the

fiendish murders of Lady Adela Ravens and her son, Bian Ravens, for which crimes he must be made to pay with his life.

– that Nicodemus Ravens thus loses and eternally forfeits every right, all goods, all titles and all inheritance and is to be known for an outlaw and a peaceless man from this time and until the day he is led to the scaffold.

– that any citizen, high or low, who aids or conceals the outlaw or refrains from assisting in his capture is deemed guilty of treason, for which misdeed said citizen may forfeit his life.

It is further made known:

– that the House of Ravens is now without lawful lord and heir.

– that the governance of Dunark Town and Castle thus falls to Drakan, blood son of Ebnezer Ravens, and hereafter **Dragonlord** of rank and name.

– that every honest man who will serve the Dragonlord faithfully and well may attain the title of **Knight of the Order of the Dragon** regardless of prior rank and standing.

The House of Ravens is down: The Order of the Dragon has risen where the Raven fell

'It's as though I am already dead . . .' whispered Nico.

'That is the way he wants it to appear,' Master Maunus said harshly. 'But you may believe that it bothers him that you are still alive. You are the stumbling block that can make *his* whole edifice collapse. Didn't you hear what Chamberlain Ossian said?'

Nico nodded. 'I did. But how many people feel the way he does? And how long will they continue to do so, with Drakan holding out this kind of threat and reward?'

'Hard to say. But the fact that he has deemed it necessary to make his announcement now shows us that he is afraid of these people and fears that their number might be growing.'

'What does he mean by that blood son stuff?' I asked. I had never heard the expression before.

'He is claiming to be the bastard son of my father,' Nico explained. 'Born outside of marriage, that is.'

'My mother has never been married. That doesn't make me a bastard!'

'Such things matter more to noble families,' said Master Maunus. 'As long as there is a lawful heir, illegitimate children have no rights.'

'But that's stupid!'

'Maybe so. But such is the law.' He put his hand on my shoulder. 'I wouldn't worry too much about it. What you have inherited from *your* mother is hardly something that can be taken away from you, is it, now?'

I closed my hand around my pendant without meaning to. Something had changed, I thought. That day in the stable when my mother had given me the pendant, I had wanted nothing more than to be rid of those damned Shamer's eyes. Now I was no longer sure that I wanted to give up the gift, even if it were possible.

'This is ridiculous,' Nico snapped. 'How can he claim to be my brother?'

Master Maunus rescued the proclamation in mid-flight as Nico made to toss it into the fire. 'Because it happens to be true.'

That silenced Nico for an instant. 'He is my cousin!'

'No. He is your half-brother.'

'But my uncle—'

'Your father was quite willing to let Dama Lizea into his bedchamber. But he did not want to marry her – that was a power he dared not give her family. And so she had to be bought off with a hastily arranged marriage to your uncle Esra – Ebnezer's own half-brother and himself a bastard, and so conveniently outside the succession.'

I thought of the dragons, which had been Dama Lizea's dowry. So that was what Master Maunus had meant when he called it a peculiar wedding.

'How do you know that?' Anger and shock had brought an ugly, mottled pallor to Nico's face.

'Because I had a hand in arranging that marriage.'

'But Drakan – he . . . all those years . . .' Nico stumbled to a stop, looking thoroughly lost.

'At the time Dama Lizea swore, as part of the arrangement, never to tell him the truth. She appears to have broken that promise.'

I was looking at the proclamation again. My thoughts were tumbling like tea leaves in a cup, tumbling and settling in new patterns. *That the House of Ravens is now without lawful lord and heir . . .*

'*That* was why,' I whispered. 'That was the reason why Bian had to die.'

'Yes,' said Master Maunus. 'That never made any sense with Nico cast as the murderer, did it? I might, just, in my wildest imaginations conceive of a Nico furious enough to get into a fight with Lord Ebnezer. But Adela and Bian? Never. Never in a million years. Drakan, on the other hand . . . If Bian were allowed to live, if Adela gave birth to her new baby – then both children would stand between him and the title. But kill the Castellan and two of his heirs and cast the blame for the murders on the third and last . . . then the House of Ravens has truly fallen, and the Order of the Dragon is free to rise.'

Nico had begun to shudder from head to foot. 'Is that it? Is that really how it was?'

'Why not? A powder of some kind in your wine – perhaps even a dose of dragon venom . . . once you were drunk enough you would hardly notice the difference. And catching you in a drunken state has not exactly been difficult lately, has it?' There was a bitter sting to the last remark, but Nico wasn't listening.

'I didn't do it,' he whispered. 'I *really* didn't do it!' He walked stiffly into the bedchamber, flung himself down on the mattress and pulled the blanket over his mouth, trying not to let us hear that he was sobbing with relief. Master Maunus and I exchanged a brief look – the first time he had ever really met my eyes – and left him in peace.

'But . . .' I began.

'But what?'

'Drakan looked me in the eye. He looked *my mother* in the eye. He killed three people and tried to get his own brother condemned for the murders – and still he looked us in the eye. How could he?'

'I don't know,' said Master Maunus. '*I* certainly wouldn't be able to.'

FOURTEEN

The Widow

Nico held up a dented metal mirror and invited me to look.

'Well?' he said. 'What do you think?'

I wasn't quite sure what to say. My hair may be as coarse as a horse's, but at least it had been thick and long, almost long enough for me to sit on. Now, there was not a hair on my head longer than a hand's span. Being so thick, it stuck out like the leaves on a bush, making me look like . . . I wasn't quite sure *what* I looked like. A troll? Some wild, fey creature raised by wolves? Not a girl, at any rate. Particularly not now that I had exchanged my dress for one of Master Maunus's woollen shirts; it reached almost to my knees, and we had had to cut off part of the sleeves; Maunus had lent me a leather belt to secure it with, making it a bit less tent-like. Luckily, I had been wearing long linen drawers, and with my calves wrapped in rags and leather thongs, they were a reasonable imitation of a boy's trousers. If no one looked too closely, I might be taken for one of the many errand boys constantly in and out through the castle gates – poor town children earning a penny or two by carrying firewood and water and suchlike for those who had the means to pay for their services.

'Call every male "sir" and everything female "good lady", no matter what rank they have. And don't look anyone in the eyes,' admonished Master Maunus.

'As long as I don't get lost,' I said nervously. 'This is not exactly my back yard.'

'Let me hear it one more time,' said the alchemist.

'Through the door and turn left. Down the first staircase I come to. Into the Arsenal Court. Down alongside the East Wing to the smithy. Through the narrow gate into Carriage Barn Alley. Across Armourer's Court and into the Stable Alley. Left through Basegate – that is, if the guards will let me. And all that is just to get out of the castle!' A bit different from home, where we could step through our front door and be on the road already.

'Once you reach the town it will be easier for you to ask directions without arousing suspicion. But if you remember my directions, you'll find the Widow's house without any trouble.'

'I don't like it,' Nico grumbled. 'What if one of the guards recognizes her?'

'In that get-up? Not very likely.' Master Maunus straightened my belt for me and inspected me with the sort of satisfied look a farmer gives a prize cow ready for the market.

'It's wrong to send a child to do a man's job,' Nico muttered darkly. 'You can't say it isn't wrong!'

'I'm nearly eleven!' I objected.

Master Maunus gave Nico his don't-be-stupid snort. 'And how far would you get before the watch caught you? How far would I get? Answer me that, Master Dunce. It is exactly *because* she is a child that she has a chance.'

'They're looking for her too!'

'They're looking for the Shamer's daughter. Does this look like the Shamer's daughter?'

'I'll be fine,' I said, less calmly than I liked. 'No one here knows me. And why would they pay any attention to some woodcutter's boy?'

'They'll pay attention all right if you look them in the eyes.' Nico's voice was razor sharp. He was angry, mostly at Master Maunus but also at himself for not being able to come up with a better plan.

'I won't do that, will I? The way Master Maunus has cut my hair it shouldn't be too difficult to avoid it.' The jagged fringe was long enough to brush the bridge of my nose. It tickled and got in the way, and I had to school myself not to push it aside every five minutes, but it hid my eyes perfectly if I bent my head even a little.

Despite Nico's objections, we followed Master Maunus's plan. I hitched the firewood basket on to my back with my good arm and stuck my left thumb through the belt so that my bad arm wouldn't dangle. The wounds had not yet healed, but they had crusted over, and the throbbing was mostly gone. But it was a good thing that the basket was empty; my legs felt rubbery from the days I had spent in bed.

'Off you go, then, Dina. The Petri Pharmacy, right

behind Saint Adela's. If she's not there, just ask for the Widow Petri. She won't have gone far.' Master Maunus smiled encouragingly. 'Don't worry. You won't get lost.'

'I hope not,' I muttered, poking my nose into the corridor. It was deserted, and I darted to the left and down the stairs. At the bottom, a guard was leaning against the wall, a thick slice of pork in his hand. Grease glistened in his beard and on his fingers. My knees felt wobbly, and not just from having been in bed for some days. But he hardly even looked at me as I clattered down the last few steps. I was just a boy with a firewood basket. I went past him, head bent and a polite 'Good morning, sir!' on my lips. He kept gnawing at his pork slice and merely nodded in acknowledgement. As I stepped out into the Arsenal Court, I had a terrible itch between my shoulder blades, expecting to hear a 'You there! Halt!' any minute, but the door swung shut behind me uneventfully.

The Arsenal Court was huge, probably the biggest yard I had ever been in, and crowded with more people and animals than I had ever seen gathered in one place before. A big octagonal building, the Arsenal, had given the courtyard its name, and behind it, at the other end of the court, was an iron fence with a gate in it. I repressed a shudder, for I knew now that that was the Dragon Gate and that beyond it lay the Pit. Apart from that and the sheer size of it, it resembled any farmyard. The noise was incredible. A flock of geese formed a waddling guard around the well, trying to keep ducks and pigeons away with furious honks and pecks. Four goats were tethered to one side, waiting to be milked, and a kid belonging to one of them had lost sight of its mother and tottered about, bleating pitifully. In one doorway stood a broad, balding man, belly wrapped in a white apron, roaring for some 'idiot brat' whom he had apparently sent off for eggs and celery; next to him, on a chain and hook, swung a dead pig with its rear end in the air and its insides in a bucket on the ground. At first glance, the pig seemed to be the only creature in the yard not yelling its head off.

I knew that standing around all agape, like a small kid who had never been to market before, was not the wisest thing to do. I had to pretend that I came here every day and knew perfectly well where I was going. But where was that smithy? Alongside the East Wing, Master Maunus had said, and then . . . yes, I could hear the clanking of the smith's hammer now. And tied to the tethering boom outside were a couple of horses, waiting to be shod. But just as I was about to turn into the narrow gate at the end of Carriage Barn Alley, a crowd of sweating men came pouring out of a black timber building, trapping me against the opposite wall. Some of them had their shirts off, but most of them wore the dark grey tunic of the watch.

'Able-bodied men, damn you,' yelled one of the tunics. 'Not any old beggar who has never held a sword before!'

'We've come to learn,' said one of the bare-chested ones, a skinny dark-haired youth. 'Regardless of prior rank and standing, it said in the proclamation. You shouldn't promise stuff like that if you don't mean it!'

'Are you calling the Dragonlord a liar?' bellowed one of the most massive of the grey tunics, shoving the dark-haired one up against the wall right next to me. I had to duck to avoid a flying arm and tried to edge away, but there were sweat-glistening bare chests and uniforms everywhere.

'Easy, Andreas,' said the first tunic in a less aggressive tone, putting his hand on the massive man's muscle-swollen arm to prevent him from shoving the dark-haired youth one more time. 'Lord Drakan is a man of his word. He has a place for any man willing to serve. But you must understand that no one is a tinker one day and a knight the next morning!'

'I'm a barrel-maker's journeyman, not a tinker.'

'Tinker or barrel-maker, a soldier you are not. But if you want to become one, you must learn to obey an order. Can you do that?'

'I suppose so.'

'Report at the Garrison Gate, then, over there behind the Arsenal. And tell them that the Weapons Master has given you the rank of novice. Do you understand?'

'Yessir,' said the barrel-maker and straightened his back. His discontent seemed to be melting away, now that he had a rank.

'And the rest – you, you and you – may go with him with the same orders.' He pointed to three more bare-chested men. Two of them came eagerly to attention like the first and began marching across the yard with a strange, stiff-legged gait that they probably imagined looked very soldierly. The effect suffered somewhat when one of them had to swerve to avoid an angry goose.

The third man remained where he was, pulling on his worn woollen jerkin. He was somewhat older than the others, balding, and with a lot of grey in his beard and in the fuzz of dark hairs on his chest.

'Novice,' he said acidly. 'Very nice. But even if those three idiots don't, *I* know that that is simply another way of saying beginner.'

'What if it is, Greybeard? We all have to start somewhere.'

'Yes. But I don't think this will be it. For me, that is.'

'You're a bit too old to take up the profession anyway, aren't you? Why did you come?'

The grey-bearded man turned his face away. 'Had me a farm and a small saddlery business down Eidin way. Then Fredin's men came. Stole most of it and burnt the rest. One of those idiots is my son. The only family I have left, now.'

'Then go and join him, Greybeard. We can always use a good harness maker.'

Greybeard nodded and headed for the Garrison. One of the grey tunics finally budged enough for me to slip out from under. None of them took the least bit of notice, despite the fact that they had me literally within reach. So far Master Maunus had been right — nobody paid attention to some raggedy kid with a basket on his back. The Weapons Master merely slapped Andreas's shoulder, a slap that echoed through the narrow alley.

'Right, let's put the next lot through their paces. It's going to be a long day!'

They disappeared into the black building again, and I hurried on down the alley. Traffic was lively. A girl my own age came towards me, leading two broad-bellied roan cows. They pushed past me, so close that the warm smooth flank of one cow rubbed against my arm. Then the alley opened up a little, and I suddenly recognized the courtyard Drakan had brought me to the first day. It had been nearly deserted, then, but at this hour it was teeming with people and animals, mostly horses, of course, as the big building on my right happened to be the Castellan's stables. I walked quickly around the stable corner, turned left and headed for Basegate, the gate that ordinary people had to use in entering or leaving the castle.

But the narrow space in front of the gate was packed with people, and I watched with a sinking heart as the watchmen carefully examined every citizen before letting him or her through the gate. A well-dressed young man had his hat snatched from his head, and a scrawny old woman was shrieking and cursing as two guards pawed through the contents of her handcart. They were clearly looking for someone, and it took no great brilliance to guess that that 'someone' was Nico. Nico, and perhaps me. I stood for a moment, nudged and pushed by the people behind me, trying to decide whether to risk it or look for another way out. Perhaps the passage through which I had come with Drakan? But that was guarded too, I knew, and besides I would end up on the sands below Dunark, and I was afraid I might never find the Widow's house from there.

I kept my place in the line and hunched my back a bit under the weight of the basket. Mama had often told us when we were ill that we might be cured more quickly by imagining ourselves to be well again. It worked on my whooping cough; might it not work on the guards as well? I squeezed my eyes shut and *imagined* that I was already through the gate, that the guards had no interest whatsoever in this small hunched-up woodcutter's boy, that . . .

'Where are you going, boy?'

My stomach had turned into stone, I was sure of it – an icy, grey, wet stone weighing about a ton. At first every thought in my head ground to a complete standstill, and I wanted simply to turn and run, but I knew that in this crowd I wouldn't get very far. And then I heard a strange voice coming out of my mouth, a snuffling, stumbling voice totally unlike my own.

'Home, sir,' I snuffled, speaking mostly through my nose. And then I knew whose voice I had borrowed; this was the way Crazy Nate talked, back home in Birches.

'You don't say,' the guard drawled. 'And just where, boy, is this home of yours?'

'With my ma.'

The shaft of his spear flicked out, rapping me sharply in the shin. 'Are you being smart with me, boy, or just stupid? Where does your mother live?'

'Home. Down by d'church.'

'Which one? Saint Adela's or Saint Magda's? Speak

119

up!' He rapped me once more with the spear, harder this time, and I thought of Crazy Nate and began sobbing and whining, pretending to be crying.

'M-m-magda's, sir. Please don't hit me n'more, sir . . .'

'Leave the lad be,' said one of the people behind me, a big, rough woman with a load of laundry on her back. 'Anyone can see he's not right in the head. Besides, the morning's getting old, and some of us've work to do.'

'Let him go, Matis,' yawned the other guard. 'It's just another of those wretched Swill Town brats who've had too many beatings and not enough meals. Or do you think this one's a lord's son?'

'Not unless the Castellan once paid a visit to the whorehouse where his mother works. Run along then, you whelp, and be quick about it.'

'Yes, sir,' I sniffled. 'Thank you, sir.'

Master Maunus was right. It was almost impossible to get lost; the spire and the peaked copper roof of the church of Saint Adela's were visible as soon as I got through the gate. Behind the church were the Apothecary Gardens, and just beyond, behind a whitewashed garden wall amid willow trees and rosehip bushes, lay the Petri Pharmacy and the Widow Petri's house. The minute I stepped through the gate in the wall I felt right at home despite the fact that I had never been there before. The smells were exactly the same as in Mama's herb garden behind Cherry Tree Cottage: the sharpness of lovage and sage, the sweeter heaviness of trumpet flower and elderberry. Bees were buzzing sleepily in the afternoon sun, gathering nectar for the last honey of the year, and in a herb bed next to the gravel path a woman was kneeling, pulling cloves of garlic from the dark brown earth. A straw hat shaded her face, held in place by a pale blue scarf.

'Madam Petri?' I asked, not certain that this was her – I had been expecting some old creature in black, seeing that everyone called her the Widow. But this woman's skirt was a mossy green, her blouse was yellow, and the shawl around her shoulders fluffy and tan like deerskin.

'Yes?' she said, straightening her back. She was also much younger than I had thought she would be. There weren't that many lines on the face below the yellow brim of the straw hat, just a furrow on either side of the mouth and a sharp little V between her brows. She might have been my mother's age; certainly, she was no ancient old hag. Wispy, golden hair clung to her sweaty forehead, and there was no grey in it that I could see.

'I have a message from Master Maunus.'

'Is that so?' She got to her feet, brushing the dirt from her skirt, and gave me a searching look. I remembered to duck my head so that she couldn't quite catch my eyes. 'Well, we had better go in, then. Bring that basket, will you?'

Easy for her to say. I had my own firewood basket, and only my left hand was free. I wasn't sure whether I could close my hand properly around the handle of the wickerwork basket; the fingers still didn't work the way I thought they should. I gripped it experimentally, but when I tried to lift it, it slipped from my grip and the garlic cloves tumbled on to the ground.

'Sorry,' I muttered, feeling myself grow hot in the face. 'I've hurt my arm.'

'Is that why he sent you to me?'

'No.' Squatting, I began to gather the garlic again.

'Leave it,' she said. 'I'll get it later.' She picked up the other basket she had filled and led the way down the gravel path and into the grey stone house she lived in.

'Sit down,' she said, indicating a blue kitchen bench. 'I'll just have a look at that arm while you tell me what the old grouch has to say to me.'

I sat down, looking around me curiously. This kitchen was both like and unlike the ones I was used to. There was a wood-stove and a work table and a pump – imagine, an indoor pump – and then there were shelves. Blue painted shelves everywhere, from the dark grey slate of the floor to the tarred beams of the ceiling. And on the shelves were jars and pots and bottles, one beside the other, more even than Master Maunus had had, before Drakan's men smashed most of them.

Using a small, neat pair of bellows, the Widow roused the embers in the stove to a cheery blaze and added a fresh log.

'Are you hungry?' she asked, pumping water into a large copper kettle. I nodded. We had been living, all three of us, off Master Maunus's normal rations. Someone might have become suspicious if he had suddenly used three times as much food as he usually did.

'So, what does he want this time?'

'I was to say that one whom the Dragon hunts needs your help.'

She paused abruptly, in the middle of a movement. A thin trickle of water continued to run from the pump for a few moments, then that, too, stopped.

'I might have guessed,' she said, very quietly. 'He was always much too fond of that boy. I hope he isn't wrong about him.'

'I was also to say that it is the Dragon himself who has cleared his own path to the top.'

She swung around, staring at me. 'Oh, so you were to say that, were you? And who are you, then, to come into my house and speak such words? Words that may cost people their lives?' She did not raise her voice, but there was a certain quality to it, something that reminded me of the sound a white-hot blade makes when the smith plunges it into a bucket of water.

'I'm Dina Tonerre,' I said, eyes on the floor. 'The Shamer's daughter.'

'*The Shamer's . . .*' Three steps brought her to my side; she seized me by the chin with one hand and pushed back my thick fringe of hair with the other. For a while she held my gaze, longer than most people could. Then she released me and sat down rather abruptly on the bench across from me.

'The Shamer's daughter,' she whispered. 'Yes. Yes, I can believe that. And you swear that Master Maunus sent you?'

'Yes. He said to say that his sister was a harridan and that her daughter is even worse.'

She smiled. 'I believe you. And as you may have

guessed . . . he is my uncle. His sister's daughter – that's me.' She rose and went to put the kettle on the stove. 'What does he want me to do?'

'I have a letter. But to get at it, we have to unwind the bandage from my arm.' Master Maunus had said that if someone searched me thoroughly enough to look there, then everything was lost anyway; no one who saw those marks would believe that I had merely been bitten by a dog.

The Widow helped me with the bandage. When she saw the large, triangular wounds, she raised an eyebrow.

'What on earth have you done to yourself?'

'It was a dragon. One of the real four-legged ones, I mean. But luckily it was almost dead, so it's not too bad.'

She gave a brief, sharp snort of disgust which sounded exactly like one of Master Maunus's. 'Not too bad – is that what he told you?'

'Actually, he said I was lucky I still had two arms.'

'I can believe that. But actually . . . it *isn't* too bad, all things considered. It's not infected, and it has crusted nicely. Be careful with that arm, though – we don't want the wounds to tear open.' She unfolded the little note that had been stuck inside the bandage. The paper looked quite blank, but the Widow seemed to know her uncle well, for without any comment she lit a taper and held the note carefully over the tiny flame until the spidery brown letters began to appear. But even that was not enough.

'The old fox. Invisible ink *and* reversed writing,' she muttered and disappeared into another room. She returned bringing a mirror, an old but beautiful one with a silver back and a handle shaped like a peacock's tail. As the kettle slowly began to hiss and steam, she read her uncle's note.

'Do you know what it says?' she asked.

'Master Maunus thought that it would be best if I didn't know too much.'

She nodded. 'He is wise to be cautious. Tell him that it can be done, but not until the day after tomorrow.'

She looked at the note one final time. Then she opened the oven door and flung the paper into the flames.

The sun had crept around to the west side of the church spire when I left the Widow's house. She had loaded my basket with firewood, as people did not often carry empty baskets into the castle. She had filled my belly too – rye bread and smoked herring and junket with apple sauce. I hadn't been that full for days. Despite the heavy load I was carrying, I felt good. I had made it past the castle guards, I had found the Widow's house without getting lost, I had remembered the message and done everything I set out to do . . . Now all that was left was to return to Master Maunus with the Widow's answer, and they probably didn't look so carefully at people going *into* the castle.

In the square by the church some pedlars had set up shop – not a big market, just a few leather goods, some pots and pans and such. A man was roasting sausages over a brazier and another was selling cider. I looked curiously at their wares as I trotted by, but no one tried to peddle anything to me. I suppose I didn't look like someone with money to spend; the tinker glared at me as if he was expecting me to try and steal something. In a way, it was nice — not being taken for a thief, of course, but the fact that for once I wasn't known to all and sundry as the Shamer's daughter. It was a strange thought that I might walk from one end of Dunark Town to the other without being noticed at all. Without hearing whispers behind my back. Without anybody crossing the street to avoid meeting my eyes. For a brief moment I was tempted to do it — just walk on, and not have to return to the castle with its massive walls and cramped hiding places and the fear of discovery. But it was just a moment. Nico and Master Maunus would be waiting for the message, probably already worrying about me. And with a bit of luck we might all get out of the castle the day after tomorrow. I had understood that much, at least, of the message I wasn't really supposed to know about.

'Do I look like a complete idiot?'

I looked up quickly, then ducked my head again. Although the cider seller's customer was practically shouting in my ear, the question wasn't meant for me. He grabbed the cider seller by the front of his shirt and hauled him halfway across the small table of his booth, so that mugs and pitchers rattled and were overturned.

'You miserable little cheat! Three shillings a mug, and then you give me short measure!'

'I never cheated anybody!' yelled the cider man, trying to wrench himself free. 'If you don't like my prices, drink somewhere else!'

The scene was already attracting a small crowd of

onlookers, but I withdrew hastily. I had seen the shiny new badge on the dissatisfied customer's short black cloak – an outline of the head of a dragon showing its fangs.

'That's no way to talk to a man of the Order of the Dragon!' he roared. 'Show some respect, you dog.'

'Order of this and order of that,' grumbled the cider seller, finally tearing himself loose from his customer's grip. 'Since when have you become so high and mighty? Last I saw, you were a bouncer at The Green Cup. What's so fine about that?'

'Maybe you haven't seen this?' He held the dragon badge under the other man's nose.

'A bit of wood and paint. What is that supposed to mean?'

'It means, my friend, that I am a Squire of the Order of the Dragon. And when I have served my time as squire, I'll be a Knight of the Dragon. And then, you little swindler, then you'll be calling me Good Sir Knight and you'll be begging to kiss my boots. Until then . . . Give me another cup and I'll consider not turning you in for giving false measure and insulting your betters!'

'God help us,' snarled the cider man in disgust. 'The paint is hardly dry and you're already sticking me for bribes? That's some kind of Order you've got! But that's how it goes. Set a beggar on horseback and he will ride to the Devil.'

'Watch your tongue, dog! You're not really badmouthing Lord Drakan, are you? You're not really an enemy of the Dragonlord – or are you?'

'No,' said the cider man, somewhat uncertainly. 'I don't suppose I am. But . . .'

'The Dragon never forgives its enemies, you know. Not like the Raven who turned a blind eye on all kinds of crimes and insults. If you want to see how the Dragon deals with traitors, come to the castle tomorrow.'

I had managed to get clear of the crowd in front of the cider stall, but that made me pause. Tomorrow? What was Drakan planning? What traitors?

'What traitors?' asked someone else in the crowd. 'Have they caught the Monster?'

The Dragon Squire shook his head. 'Not yet. But they have the witch – the false Shamer who is in league with him.'

False Shamer? Witch? Was that my mother he meant?

'What witch? What are you talking about?' I cried.

'It ought to be quite a show,' said the squire, obviously enjoying the attention of the crowd. 'The false Shamer, the one that tried to get them to release the Monster . . . She has been convicted of witchcraft and treason and is to be executed tomorrow. You should come and see it.'

'Why?' said the tinker. 'I've no intention of missing out on nearly a whole day's trade just to see some poor woman hang.'

'Oh, they're not going to hang her,' said the squire, smiling expectantly. 'She will be torn to pieces and eaten. They're letting one of the dragons have her.'

I couldn't move. I couldn't breathe. There was a strange kind of roaring in my ears, and I had begun to shake all over. I knew now where my mother was.

Drakan had her. And tomorrow he would give her to the dragons.

'Well?' said the squire, holding out his mug. 'Can a man get some service around here?'

The cider seller didn't say a word. He just picked up his ladle, dipped it in the barrel, and filled the squire's cup to the brim.

FIFTEEN

Chaining a Dragon

I still don't remember how I got from the cider stall and back to the castle. I'm not even sure if I was stopped at the gate or not. If I was, I must have seemed weirder than Crazy Nate; I doubt I made much sense. I think there was so much going on inside my head that I simply couldn't take too much notice of what was happening outside. It's something of a miracle that I managed to find my way back.

I remember sitting by the fireplace in Master Maunus's workshop, feeling cold to the marrow despite the heat of the flames. I remember Nico and Master Maunus arguing. Nico ended up shouting so loudly that Master Maunus had to hush him, or we would have had the watch at the door. After that they fought on in peculiar hushed tones that didn't fit the words.

'If you think I'm going to run off and save my own hide while that fiend feeds Dina's mother to his disgusting worms, then you are very much mistaken!'

'Have you completely taken leave of your senses, boy? Can't you *see* it's a trap?'

'So? What are we to do, send him a letter? "Dear Drakan, we know it's a trap and we're not falling for it, so will you please not kill Dina's mother?" He's sure to release her right away, don't you think?'

'Settle down, boy, you're acting like a madman—'

'Oh? Better than acting like a coward!'

'Would you please use whatever brains the Almighty has seen fit to give you? Just for a moment? If you put yourself within Drakan's grasp and let him feed *you* to the dragons instead, what have we gained? Do you think he will release the Shamer then? Or the Shamer's daughter? Or me? Or the Widow?'

'I would never reveal—'

'Not of your own free will and perhaps not for a good while. But eventually he would have it out of you, because he wouldn't stop, he would never stop until he had dug out and seized every last one of his opponents. Not that there would be that many to oppose him. Not with you gone. *Then* the House of Ravens really would have fallen and there would be nobody to tell the truth he struggles to keep hidden: that *Drakan* is the murderer, that *he* is the real Monster. Think, boy. Think!'

'You're always saying that. And you're so very good at it too, aren't you? Whatever the crime, you can always *think* of a reason not to *do* anything about it! But sometimes, Master, only cowards do not act!'

Master Maunus's normal ruddiness blanched to an angry pallor. For a while he made no answer, and his silence brooded in the room like a big black bird. Then he turned his back on Nico and stared into the fire, as if he had lost something in the dancing flames.

131

'You must do as you see fit,' he said tonelessly. 'I am not your Master any more. But let Dina carry a message to the Widow, at least, so that you do not needlessly endanger more lives.'

'Again?' Nico spoke more quietly now that Maunus had given in. 'Isn't that a little risky?'

'You think, perhaps, that she is safer here? Once you begin to play the hero, no place inside the castle walls is safe for her. It's better that she goes to the Pharmacy and stays there until . . . until it's over.'

It was obvious that he had changed his mind in mid-sentence. What had he intended to say? Until what? Until my mother was dead? Until Nico had been caught? It was hard to imagine happier endings right now.

'That's probably a good idea,' said Nico. 'Dina, you had better stay with the Widow.'

I merely nodded. Nico looked surprised – perhaps he had expected me to object. But I didn't want to get into an argument with him now, and it was easier just to pretend that I would do as he said.

'Give me another note or whatever message you want her to have,' I said. 'If I am to go, it must be now, before they close the castle gates for the night.'

They were both looking at me with funny expressions.

'Are you all right?' asked Master Maunus. 'How is your arm?'

'I'm fine. Give me the message.'

'Maybe you should have a cup of tea first,' said Nico. 'You don't seem quite yourself. It must have been awful,

132

hearing . . . what they said about your mother.'

I got to my feet. There was no comfort in the heat of the fire anyway, it was better to be up and doing. And I had had just about enough of their endless quarrelling.

'I would rather go now.'

The guard on the stairs was a different one, which was probably lucky for me. The pork eater might have wondered a bit to see the same firewood boy pass so many times in one day. The new one stood in the doorway, straining his neck to catch a glimpse of something going on out there in the Arsenal Court. He barely noticed me edging past.

'Damn,' he said. 'You can hardly see it, what with the crowd and all.'

I looked across the yard, and there was quite a throng of people gathered at the other end.

'See what, sir?' I asked cautiously.

'The dragon,' he said. 'They're chaining it – so that it'll be ready for tomorrow.'

I began to walk across the courtyard. I don't know why. Why on earth would I want to see the dragon picked to kill my mother? But I did. So maybe Nico was right when he said that I didn't seem quite myself.

At first I could see nothing except broad adult backs. I caught the smell, though, the stench of rotting meat that I knew far too well. Then there was a sound, a thin bleat that certainly wasn't made by any dragon. I eeled my way through the crowd, taking no notice of the shoves and harsh words that came my way. When I finally got to the front, I could see that the guards had tied a small, piebald goat kid to the fence surrounding part of the Dragon Pit. The kid tore desperately at the tether, trying to get free. No wonder. On the other side of the fence, two of the monsters were approaching, waddling and slithering towards the little goat; one hissed at the other and threw itself forward, trying to get there first. They were a lot faster in the late afternoon sun than they had been in the cold of the night. A good thing too, or both Nico and I would have ended up as dragons' dinner.

The kid's bleating grew even more frantic, and it leaped and fought so hard that the tether flipped it on to its back. Someone in the audience laughed, but I had a sour, sickening taste in my mouth. I wanted to rush over there and cut the terrified animal loose, but I didn't quite dare. The two dragons snapped at each other, fangs glinting. Neither of them wanted to give up the prey to the other, and the fenced opening wasn't big enough for both of them. The biggest one managed to close its jaws around the other's front leg, forcing it to withdraw, hissing and limping. The bigger dragon now pushed itself against the fence, trying to get at the kid; but at first it couldn't force its head through the bars, no matter how hard it tried.

'The wicket! Now!' roared one of the guards at the top of his lungs, and two of his assistants pulled on a lever, raising a part of the gate. The dragon immediately thrust its head through, sinking its fangs into the kid's flank. The little goat screamed pitifully and blood began to stain its piebald flanks; yet for a moment it actually succeeded in breaking free. The dragon struck again.

This time, it caught the kid by the head, and after that there were no more screams, though the hind legs continued to kick spasmodically for a while.

'The chain!' commanded the man who seemed to be in charge, and while the dragon still had its mouth full of kid, a very brave guard threw a heavy chain around its neck and tightened it. The dragon flung its head up and tried to reach him with its claws, but the wicket opening was too narrow, and he succeeded in getting a lock on the chain before the dragon thought of backing up into the wider space behind it.

'Man's got guts,' muttered one of the onlookers, a heavy-set man with a bright new dragon badge on his tunic. 'They would have to pay me an awful lot of money to do what he just did!'

'They say he's getting ten silver marks,' said the man next to him. 'Ten silvers! Imagine that – my whole family could live on that for half a winter!'

There was a squealing, grating sound of gears rarely used; an iron grille descended behind the dragon, closing off the entrance to the Pit, and the Dragon Gate itself began to open. The monster shook its head, spattering the dragon tamer with goat's blood. He wiped his face with an irritated motion and put some distance between himself and the beast. The dragon took a few waddling steps forward, into the courtyard, and suddenly no one in the crowd was in such a hurry to push forward. As a matter of fact, there was a general backwards shuffle, and I found myself more or less alone in the front.

I should have pulled back, too, but I stood still instead,

watching the dragon. I looked at it, at its scaly grey legs, its yellow eyes and the bloody bits of goat dangling from its jaws. It wasn't like that time in the Pit when I had been so paralysed with fear that Nico had had to force me to move on. I think I was just trying to understand – understand that Drakan had put all this in motion, the kid, the chain, the dragon tamer and his ten silver marks, because he was actually going to do it. He really was going to give my mother to the dragon and let it kill her as though she were a goat.

'Better be careful,' said a voice behind me, and a hand fell on my shoulder. I spun around and looked up. The hand belonged to a castle guard who had apparently been detailed to make sure people stayed at a safe distance. 'They're venomous, you know, and it might spit at—' He broke off. I realized that I was looking him in the eye and hurriedly lowered my glance.

'I won't get too close,' I said. 'And anyway, I had best be off home . . .' I ducked out from under his hand and tried to look like a boy in a hurry to get home.

'Wait . . .' The guard reached for me again. He sounded confused rather than commanding, though, as if he wasn't quite sure himself why he wanted me to stop.

'My ma will be mad if I'm late,' I called over my shoulder and began to push my way through the crowd.

The guard made no answer, and I fervently hoped he would never realize why it had bothered him so to look a woodcutter's boy in the eyes. I was out of the crowd now and trotting purposefully towards Carriage Barn Alley. Once I was out of sight, he would no doubt forget about me, and in another few paces . . .

'Halt! You there, with the basket, stay where you are!'

My heart was pounding again, but I pretended not to hear the order. Just a few more paces and I would be out of his sight.

'Andreas, stop him!'

There was a movement behind me. I threw a quick look over my shoulder, and there was the brawny guard from that morning, the one who had been so ready to thump the newcomers wanting to be Knights. And although he was big, he was quick on his feet. One minute he was easing himself off the black timber wall, the next I was struggling in the grip of a very large and hairy-backed hand.

'Where do you think you're going?' he said, clutching me by the shirt and dragging me into the black building with one mighty heave. The fabric of the shirt gave way with a tearing sound, and I dropped the basket and ended up on my hands and knees on the dusty clay floor. A flash of pain shot up my arm, but I didn't even have time to wince. Grabbing me by the nape of the neck, he pulled me to my feet again. 'Didn't you hear the order? When a guard cries "Halt!", you stop, brat.'

I know now how a rat feels when Beastie has it by the scruff. The Brawn was gripping me so hard that I could think of little else. I think my feet actually left the ground, or maybe it was just my knees buckling.

'Have a care, Andreas. He's just a boy.'

'He's old enough to try to run from Hannes,' said Andreas. But he let go of me, and I tumbled to the floor once more.

'I see,' said my rescuer, and I saw that it was the Weapons Master from that morning. The building appeared to be a training practice hall for the castle watch. Everywhere on the tarred black timber walls hung armour and weaponry, staffs, spears, clubs, helmets, mail shirts and swords. 'And what does Hannes want with this pipsqueak?'

'I don't know,' said Andreas. 'But the boy wouldn't stop when he was told.'

At that moment the other guard appeared in the doorway. 'So, you got him,' he said, pulling at his tunic which had hiked up somewhat from his run.

'If that's what you want to call it. What do you want him for?' Pulling off his helmet, the Weapons Master ran a hand through his short brown hair, which looked sticky with sweat.

'I'm not sure . . .' said Hannes sheepishly. 'There's something about him . . .'

'Something about him,' repeated the Weapons Master scornfully. 'My God, that's terrible. We'd better throw him in the clink right away.'

Hannes looked even more sheepish, but he persevered.

'I think I've seen him before somewhere, or . . . well, he *reminds* me of someone.'

The Weapons Master sighed. 'Get up, boy. Why wouldn't you stop?'

I took my time getting to my feet and hung my head as if shy or ashamed. 'I wasn't sure he meant me, and . . . I promised Ma I'd be home early.'

'A criminal mastermind, I see.' The Weapons Master

gave Hannes a look of disgust. 'See if he's pinched anything, and if he hasn't, let him go. Damn it, man, we have better things to do!'

'I'm not a thief!' I said, as indignantly as I dared. 'I didn't steal anything!'

Andreas pushed me up against the wall and pinned me there with one hand, dragging Master Maunus's leather belt off me with the other. He threw the belt to Hannes, who loosened the string of my leather purse and poured the contents into his hand.

'Four copper pennies, a bit of bread, a note, and some lint,' he said.

'What does the note say?' asked Andreas.

'Er . . . I'm not too good with letters . . .'

'Let me see that.' The Weapons Master took the note. 'One cord of firewood, paid in full: four coppers,' he read.

'It's called a receipt,' I said. 'So that Mistress Curran can tell I'm not cheating.'

This time, I thought Master Maunus had been even cleverer than last time. He had written the message in invisible ink – and then written the bit about the firewood on top of it, so that I wouldn't be carrying a mysteriously blank note.

Hannes was staring at the four coppers, but I didn't think he really saw them. One could almost feel the cogs in his mind turning over. He knew there *was* something more to this seemingly innocent woodcutter's boy. But he couldn't figure out what. 'Give the boy his purse back and let him go,' said the Weapons Master, and relief made me weak at the knees. Andreas let go of me, and Hannes gave me back the purse and belt. My hands shook as I fastened the buckle.

'Better have this back too, boy,' said the Weapons Master, holding out the note. 'So that Mistress Curran can tell you're not cheating.'

'Thank you, sir,' I said, reaching for it.

He did not let go.

We stood there, both of us holding on to the paper, and I couldn't understand why he didn't let go.

'Sir?' I said, my voice trembling a little. 'May I have my note back?' I was careful not to raise my eyes.

'Your hands are too clean,' he said.

At first I didn't get it. It was so unexpected. So upside down. Your hands are dirty, Mama would say. And then I would have to go to the pump and wash them before I was allowed to touch the food or her jars and bottles or whatever it was. No one, I thought, had ever before told me that my hands were too *clean*.

And then I realized what was wrong. I pictured the hands of the miller's boys, or Crazy Nate's – broad, strong paws, rough and broken-nailed, with dirt encrusted in every line and crack, so that it looked like they had been marked up with brown ink. I let go of the paper and pulled back, but it was too late, of course. The Weapons Master seized my wrist and held on to it.

'This was never a boy's hand,' he said. 'And certainly not a firewood boy's.'

I tried to break free, but all that effort yielded was a jarring pain in my bad arm, as Andreas grabbed hold of my left elbow. I had to bite my lip to keep from crying out.

'Are you saying that . . . that this is a girl?'

The Weapons Master put his thumb under my chin and forced me to raise my face.

'Take a proper look at her,' he said. 'Of course it's a girl.'

I closed my eyes, but I could feel the tears welling up to bead my lashes. The arm Andreas was holding was throbbing and burning, and the thought that I had come so close to escaping and had still been caught . . . all in all, it was close to unbearable.

'Look at me,' coaxed the Weapons Master softly. 'Look at me, my girl . . .' As though I were some animal he was attempting to train.

All right, I thought. He asked for it. Let him have it. And I opened my eyes and caught his glance.

'*Let go of me,*' I said in my best Shamer's voice. '*Is this how you treat those weaker than yourselves?*'

They let go of me, both of them. I backed towards the door. Andreas was shaking his head from side to side, as if someone had caught him a blow with a hammer. The Weapons Master merely stood. His glance wandered, but kept returning to me.

'You're the Shamer's daughter,' he said.

'Yes. And now you want to feed me to the dragons too, I suppose? And make a show of it, so people will *pay* to come and see it?' I couldn't quite manage the Voice, there was too much fury and too much uncertainty in it. But the Weapons Master lowered his eyes all the same.

'We won't hurt you,' he said. 'And perhaps you and your mother will both be able to go free soon. If the real murderer is caught.'

'Do you even know who that is? Have you even thought about—'

I got no further. Hannes seized me from behind and put his hand on my mouth.

'I've got her,' he shouted.

I sank my teeth into his hand.

'Ow!' he yelled. 'She bit me! That devil brat bit me!'

'And I hope you *die* from it,' I screamed, kicking his shin. But although he cursed a streak, he would not let go of me, and Andreas had come to life again now. He tore some old cloak off a hook on the wall and threw it over my head. I couldn't see and I could barely breathe. One of them, Hannes I think, kicked my feet from under me and pinned me to the floor with what felt like a knee in my back.

'Give me your belt,' growled Andreas, and shortly afterwards something tightened around me, cloak and all, making it impossible for me to move my arms. The knee went away, but I still couldn't get up. The cloak had a mouldy, filthy smell and was so thick that it felt as if I was suffocating. The belt they had used to secure it was cutting into my injured arm, and something, probably Andreas's grip, had caused the wounds to tear open; a warm, wet stain was spreading from elbow to wrist. Laboriously, I rolled over on my good side, trying to get my feet under me.

'She bit me!' Hannes repeated, in a frightened voice. 'I'm bleeding . . .'

'Go and hold it under the pump awhile,' said the Weapons Master.

'But she . . . do you think . . . I mean, she *cursed* me.'

'So? Are you expecting to drop dead? She doesn't have venom fangs, for God's sake. Go and rinse it. Andreas, you take the girl. I think we have to go and see the high command about this.'

Andreas dragged me to my feet by hauling on the belt. Then I was suddenly upside down as he threw me over his shoulder like some travel pack. I wriggled, trying to get down, but he just growled at me.

'Stop that,' he said. 'We can easily tie up your legs as well.'

I stopped wriggling. I felt helpless enough as it was.

Andreas carried me like a rolled-up rug, and dropped me like a rolled-up rug. I couldn't see and I couldn't break my fall, and although the heavy cloak cushioned me somewhat, I still hit my shoulder and my knee and suffered another hot wave of pain from my arm.

'Well,' said a cool voice. 'What is this object?'

'A girl, Medama. We've caught the Shamer's daughter.'

'And why is she wrapped up like some Midwinter Gift?'

'Medama, we thought . . .' The Weapons Master paused, clearing his voice uncomfortably. 'Her eyes, Medama . . .'

'She is a child, Weapons Master. I feel confident that three grown men will be enough to control her – even with her face free. Release her.'

I'm not quite sure who I had expected this 'high

command' to be. But when Andreas loosened the belt and that suffocating cloak was gone at last, I found myself looking at voluminous blue silk skirts. And as I raised my head, my eyes fell on a gold-embroidered bodice, black hair caught firmly in a net of white pearls, and finally, slowly – for this time, I was the one reluctant to look – on a deathly pale skull-like face. Lady Death. Dama Lizea. Drakan's mother.

It was unreal. Inside my head, confused images flurried – a knife, a blizzard of white down, those furious screams so shrill they sounded more like a hawk's than a human's. She bent over me, and I cringed without meaning to. But all she did was touch my sleeve gently.

'You are bleeding, child. Have they hurt you?'

I could hardly believe my own ears. Here I was, half expecting her to bring out a knife and finish me off then and there. And there *she* was, sounding as if she genuinely cared about my bitten arm. Surprise made me numb.

Her skeletal white hand pushed back my sleeve, exposing the soggy bandage.

'We didn't do that,' said the Weapons Master.

'Probably the monster injured her.' Dama Lizea let the sleeve drop. 'Poor child. You were lucky to get away from him before he did worse. And now you are safe.'

I opened my mouth, only to close it again. I wanted to defend Nico, but it didn't seem the smart thing to do. Above all, I must not let on that I knew where he was.

'You are quite overwhelmed, are you not? Here – sit in this chair. What is it they call you?'

'Dina,' I croaked, feeling as if someone had dumped me in some magic castle where everyone did the opposite of what you would expect them to do. Why was she being so nice? Was it because the Weapons Master and his men were there? She took my good elbow and supported me as if afraid that I would fall. The chair she wanted me to sit in had a seat of red leather and a cushion of brocade glinting with gold thread. It was certainly never designed for a backside as ragged and dirty as mine.

'Tell us what happened, Dina,' she said. 'How did you get away? Where did he hold you captive?'

Her perfume hovered around me like an invisible cloud, almost as stifling as the cloak had been. I did not know what to answer. I decided to try a question instead.

'Where is my mother? Why do you want to kill her? She has done nothing wrong!' I tried to catch her eyes, but she looked at the Weapons Master, as if he was the one she was talking to.

'Your mother has given false evidence and has betrayed her office,' she said. 'These are serious crimes. But perhaps she has done it out of fear for your life. Now that we may show her that you are safe in our care, I hope she will change her testimony. And if you were to help us catch Nicodemus-the-monster . . . well, I think she might escape punishment altogether.'

She had stepped back from me a little and would not look at me directly, but I could sense her observing me all the same, gauging my reactions. She stood to one side of the chair, resting one hand on its back and the other on my shoulder. I knew what she was waiting for

– she had as much as said so: Give us Nico, and you and your mother will go free.

For some reason Cilla came to mind. Cilla and that day in the miller's barn when we had played Court-the-Princess. I had misjudged Cilla that day, though I had known her all my life and thought I knew what to expect from her. And Cilla with her pink sheet and her crown of ox-eye daisies – she was nothing but a poor imitation. This was the real Princess, smooth and shiny on the surface with silk skirts and pearls to rival the glitter of her smile, but lethal to any poor wretch who stumbled in her game. The knife had been a real knife, and the thought of what they would do to Nico if they found him made me sick to my stomach.

I didn't trust her. She probably knew that I would do just about anything to save my mother. I could still remember the scrunch of the dragon's jaws closing around the head of the kid. But *if* I swapped Nico's life for Mama's – I couldn't even be sure that she would keep her part of the bargain. And Nico . . . I thought of how he had wanted to drink Drakan's wine that night in the cell, even knowing it was poisoned. How he had fought so hard to be brave, and how he still couldn't help being afraid, afraid of the executioner's sword, afraid of dying surrounded by crowds of people who would yell and scream and hate him, because they thought he had killed a woman, a child, and an old man.

I could feel Dama Lizea's bony fingers on my shoulder. If only she wouldn't touch me. My arm throbbed and the wet stain was spreading, soaking the entire sleeve. I had no idea whether it was right or wrong, clever or extremely stupid. But I snapped my head around so quickly that she had no time to look away.

'***Tell us why your son killed Bian***,' I said. The child. The child had to be the worst, I thought, if she had any kind of conscience at all.

Her eyes were a blue so dark it was nearly black. Her face was completely expressionless, but for a moment I felt her fury as keenly as though it were my own.

'The Castellan,' she hissed. 'He gave me away, as though I were a horse or a hound. Gave me away, once he had tired of me . . . and *my* son was not good enough for the Castellan's Seat, oh no, we cannot have a *bastard* on the throne . . . What we did was justice, that is all . . . Justice!'

And then her face was not expressionless any more. She shoved me away from her, so hard that the chair fell over and I went down on one knee.

'Devil's spawn!' she cried. 'Weapons Master, seize her! She is as false as her mother – just as false, and just as dangerous!'

She turned her back on me and buried her face in her hands. Her thin shoulders were shaking. Was she crying? The Weapons Master and Hannes and Andreas were all standing there like statues, staring at her. Had they heard what she said? Had she even said it out loud, or did you have to be a Shamer to hear it? Perhaps it was just my question that had turned them into stone.

'Did you not hear me?' snapped Dama Lizea, her voice slightly more controlled now. 'Seize that witch's brat before she puts a spell on us all.'

SIXTEEN

The Ice Girl

Later, I would sometimes dream about it. Waking up in the darkness, still unable to see, I would feel for a moment the pressure of the rough blindfold they used. And for a moment, too, I would be able to smell Lady Death and her sickening mixture of heavy, sweet perfume and the stench of dragon's blood.

Her tender concern for my arm came to a quick end. They had no care for that when they bound my hands and hauled me along to some place I never saw. It was cold there, and the floor was stone, hard and smooth like marble. It smelled of ash and soap and dampness. Not a cell, I thought, or not at least to anyone but me. Somewhere a steady dripping – perhaps a bathhouse of some kind? But not a simple wooden shed like ours by the Cherry Tree stream; here, voices echoed, bouncing back from walls of stone. The voices weren't the Weapons Master's, or Hannes's or Andreas's. They were unknown to me, and faceless, because I couldn't see.

'So you want to see the dragon eat your mother? We'll make sure you get a good seat.'

'We'll let you get really close. Close enough to be spattered by her blood.'

Something wet hit me in the face; I breathed in some of it and had to cough and snort. The voices were making pictures in my head, pictures so vivid that at first I thought it really was blood. For a moment I even smelled the heavy stench I knew from the miller's slaughterhouse. It took a few seconds before I recognized the taste and scent of wine.

'Your mother is a witch, they say. But one would have thought her own child cared for her a little, all the same.'

'Don't you love her? Don't you?'

Hands seized me and shoved me against a wall, shaking me so that my head thudded against the smooth stone wall.

'*What kind of child doesn't love her mother?*' The roar echoed, washing over me like a moist gust of wind, a gust full of wine breath and little droplets of spit.

'Do you want to hear what it will sound like when the dragon tears her up? Do you? It sounds like this!' A wet sort of crunch by my ear, like the sound it makes when one pulls the leg off a fried chicken.

It was too much.

I felt a jagged cramp in my stomach, and a thin, acid squelch of vomit invaded my mouth. I spat, and spat again, hoping to hit them, wishing I could spit out the pictures too, the horrible pictures they were making in my mind, pictures that wouldn't come *out*.

'Let go of me,' I cried, more sob than shout. 'Let me go, let me go, let me go . . .' and then it wasn't a shout at all, just sobbing.

'Let her go.' A new voice, one that hadn't been saying any of the horrible things. And the one who had been shaking me did let me go. I lost my balance and fell to the floor, but this time someone, the new voice, I thought, steadied me and held me.

'Don't be so rough on her,' he said, holding me gently while I cried. 'It's not her fault. *She* didn't kill three innocent people.'

I was sitting partly on the floor, partly on his lap, completely unable to stop crying. He stroked my hair like my mother might have done. Or perhaps my father, whom I had never known.

'There,' he mumbled. 'Everything will be better now. Your mother will be free. You will be free. No one will be eaten by the dragon.'

My body relaxed without asking permission from me. It let itself be held and comforted, and I actually believed him. Everything would be better. The bad times were over now.

'It's not your fault,' he whispered, his lips so close that I could feel his breath on my neck. 'It's his fault. His fault, all of it. And as soon as we know where he is, everything will be all right again.'

My body still wanted to be rocked and held. In my head, horrible and bloody images churned, and I wanted them to stop. I wanted everything to be the way it used to be. Mama, Davin, Melli and me. Before Drakan. Before Nico. I was furious with Nico, and I really hated him for tearing everything apart and putting it together again in such terrible new ways. It was his fault that I had been put to this choice. Nico *or* Mama. Mama *or*

Nico. How had the world come to be like this? It was actually Nico's fault, just like the man said.

'Tell us,' he whispered. 'So that we can take this blindfold off and untie your hands. Where is he?'

I came so close. So close. It was so hard not to tell. But although she had said not a word, although she stood quite still pretending not to be there, I could smell her. Lady Death. And I thought of Cilla, and of not trusting people even when they smiled.

'I don't know,' I sniffled. 'I really don't!'

'Where did you see him last?'

'In the passage by the Dragon Pit. He wouldn't take me with him. He said he had to get out of town, and that I would just be in his way. He didn't want me with him . . .' It wasn't hard to cry, or to sound hurt and angry.

'What did you do? Where did you get those clothes?'

'I . . . I stole them off a washing line. But I'm not a thief. I've never taken anything before, really I haven't! I found this woman who needed someone to carry wood for her customers. She pays me a ha'penny for every basket I carry. I thought . . .' I sniffled again, 'I thought I would be able to pay someone to take me home. But everything's so expensive here!'

'And your mother? Were you just going to leave her here?'

'I didn't know . . . until this afternoon I didn't know that she . . . that you . . .'

'That she had been arrested?'

'Yes. I didn't know that.'

For a while there was silence. Then he pushed me away, not harshly or violently, but still firmly enough to cause a stab of pain in my arm. A door opened and closed. Then silence again. Was I alone? I couldn't tell. I just sat there on the hard floor, feeling shivery and small and scared and hurting all over. I didn't know if they believed me. Maybe that was what they had gone outside to discuss.

The door opened again. Footsteps reached me.

'Do you hear me?' It was Dama Lizea's voice, low and harsh. Her smell enveloped me. 'Do you hear me, witchling?'

'Yes . . .' I whispered, not daring to defy her.

'Your mother dies tomorrow, witch brat. Your mother dies, and the monster will still be walking, eating, drinking and breathing long after she is just a bit of bloody meat and a few splinters of bone. Is that what you want? Does that make you happy?'

I think it was then that I turned to ice. I can explain it no better. It wasn't that my body stopped bleeding and throbbing and hurting. It just didn't seem to matter any more. It was as if I had found some place in my head, very far away from everything. Beneath my ordinary warm skin I had become a statue, a girl of ice, hard and clear and motionless.

She was waiting. But the ice girl didn't feel like talking. I said nothing. Then she suddenly blew down her nose, as if at some unpleasant smell, and drew back a bit; I heard her silk skirts rustle.

'She is filthy. She stinks. Hose her down and throw her out. I will no longer tolerate such devil's spawn in my house.'

They must have been ready and waiting. I had no

152

time even to duck my head. Icy cold water washed over me from behind, from in front and finally from above. Three huge bucketfuls, and I was as soggy as a drowned mouse. Again, I was dragged by my bound arms, but not as far this time. Up a few stone steps and through a door, into cold night air; and then I was pushed to my knees on some uneven peaked cobbles.

'Farewell, witch brat,' snarled one of the faceless voices. 'I feel sorry for your mother!' Sharp steel nicked the skin on my wrist but also cut the cords, and my arms flopped forwards, free at last but limp and useless like a rag doll's from having been bound so long. A final shove sent me down on my belly on the cobbles, cold and damp from the night air.

For a long time I lay there, waiting for the next blow. I heard footsteps receding, but I wasn't sure they were all gone. The silence went on. The dragon arm still refused to obey me, but a bit of life and movement returned to the other one, and I got myself into a sitting position. Stiff-fingered, I pried at the blindfold. I couldn't undo the knots, and the cloth was tied so tightly that I couldn't pull it down past my nose. Finally I managed to push it up on my forehead, so that I could see again.

I was sitting in the middle of the Arsenal Court. The moon hung above the spire on the West Wing, and not a single person, man or woman, guard or palace maid, was to be seen. In the shadow beneath the Dragon Gate, not thirty paces away, lay the chained dragon, coiled like a snake in a basket. The ice girl coldly considered the possibility of killing it now, while the chill of the night made it slow and torpid, but I had no spear and probably not enough strength for the task, either. In any case, there were more dragons in the Pit. They could just get a new one.

I got up. My legs felt cold and clumsy. The only part of me not chilled was the dragon arm, which continued to burn and throb as if I had acquired a second heart there. I started walking through the court on feet I couldn't feel. At the well I paused and drank from the horse trough, not feeling strong enough to haul a fresh bucket from the depths. The water was icy and tasted vaguely of stone and moss, but despite being wet all over, I was desperately thirsty and drank for a long time.

Once I had drunk enough for my stomach to feel bloated with water, I walked on down Carriage Barn Alley. I didn't really have a plan. My head felt clear but still. I didn't think of the gate watch at all, though they were bound to stop a dripping wet pauper boy with no basket or firewood for disguise. But when I reached the gate, the guard was sprawled against it, apparently fast asleep, and the little wicket had been left open. And so I continued out of the gate and into the sleeping town.

The only person I knew was the Widow, and even through the ice inside I felt a stab of longing for the blue-painted kitchen and the warmth of her woodstove. *The Petri Pharmacy, right behind Saint Adela's. Don't worry. You won't get lost.* Saint Adela's' spire stood like a black needle against the sky, moonlight glittering on the gold ball at the top of it. I padded along in my wet boots, making strange squishy sounds at every step. Would she be mad at me for disturbing her so late? No, not the Widow. She would sit me down on the blue kitchen bench and put the big copper kettle on. Maybe she would take off my wet clothes and lend me her warm, brown deerskin shawl instead, and there would be such wonderful smells in the kitchen, of camomile, elderberry, and willow-bark tea, just like the kitchen smells in Cherry Tree Cottage when Mama . . .

My fantasy came to a grinding halt. Mama was not in the kitchen at Cherry Tree Cottage and might never be there again. It was like a blow, a blow that shattered the ice inside me and made me stumble and drop. I broke the fall with my hands and paid for it with a blinding stab of pain from the dragon arm. And it was while I knelt there on the cobbles, holding my burning, throbbing arm, that I heard it. At first I took it for an echo of my own footsteps. But this was a different sound, drier and more cautious than my wet squelching.

I got to my feet and half turned. There was nothing behind me, only moonlit cobbles and shadowed walls. And none of the shadows was moving.

Maybe I was imagining things. I rested against a wall for a few breaths, listening hard. I could hear only my own breathing and the distant barking of an angry dog, several streets away.

I started forward again, this time listening as I walked. There it was again — a low, careful tiptoeing, stopping when I stopped, moving when I moved.

I turned down alongside the church of Saint Adela's and crossed the square where the cider seller had had his stall. The Widow's house was now so close that I could smell the herbs in her garden. Oh, how I longed to stop. How I longed to rest on the bench by the stove and let her deal with everything else. But there were the footsteps behind me. And the conveniently sleeping guard at the gate . . . and Lady Death, who was far from stupid but might think that I was. I could almost hear them discussing it, while I had been lying blind and bound on the other side of the bathhouse door. Let her go, they would have said. Let her go and let us see where she runs to!

So as I came to the gate in the whitewashed wall around the Widow's garden, I went past it. I walked on, down an unfamiliar street, away from the church square and into this strange town where I knew no other soul.

SEVENTEEN

Footsteps and Shadows

I didn't know whether there was one person or several. Sometimes I could almost believe that there wasn't anybody. Perhaps it had been a cat or a dog, or someone who just happened to be going my way for a while. Oh, if only that was true! Then I would be able to turn around, right now, and go back to the Widow's house – if I could still find it. The streets wandered this way and that, narrow and unfamiliar, and I could no longer see the spire of Saint Adela's.

Nearly all the houses were dark and shuttered; only one place on this street showed signs of life. It was a tavern. A square of light fell on the cobbles from the open door, like a promise of warmth and companionship, and I stopped without really deciding to. But the landlord was preparing to shut his doors too, getting rid of the last of his customers. Some of them complained loudly, calling him a lazy dog and a piss-ant little beer-pedlar who wouldn't even let a man enjoy the drink he'd paid for. One of the loudest complainers wore a shiny new dragon badge on his shirt, which cured me of any notion of moving closer. Instead, I turned into an alley hardly wide enough for a handcart and was then forced to stop again. In the middle of the alley stood a woman straddling the gutter in a peculiar manner, with her rough black skirts spread as far as they would go. At first I couldn't think what she might be doing, but then I heard it. She was peeing, and by the sound of it, peeing hard enough to make a horse jealous. It seemed the sort of thing one shouldn't interfere with, so I stood hesitantly behind her for some moments. While I was still hesitating, she finished, shook herself a bit and walked on as if nothing had happened.

'Excuse me . . .' I said quietly. 'Excuse me, good lady!'

She turned around slowly. The slowness was probably due to some difficulty in controlling her legs – at any rate, I could smell the gin on her from seven paces away.

'Who're you calling lady?' she asked. 'Me?'

I nodded silently. On closer inspection, nothing much about her was very ladylike. Her bodice had come undone at the top and was so speckled with stains that it looked as if it might have been made from fishskin. Her hair had probably begun the day in a tidy bun, but now it was half up, half down, and sticking damply to her neck. She wore neither shawl nor cloak despite the chill of the night.

'Well at least you've got manners. But run along. I'm skint, and even if I had a penny I'd've better uses for it.'

'No, that's not it,' I said quickly. 'If only the lady would tell me . . . I just want to know where the church is.'

'The church? Straight on, through the gate, turn right, and you'll see it.'

'Thank you, good lady,' I said, edging past her. 'Goodnight.'

'Hey,' she yelled after me. 'Won't do you no good, that. They lock their doors just like everybody else these days . . .'

I went straight, through the gate, turned right, and there it was – the church. Only one thing wrong: it wasn't Saint Adela's. This was a different building, heavier and darker-looking, grey and black in the moonlight. An iron fence encircled it, with sharp points at the top like spears. Between the fence and the church walls the gravestones jostled each other, the town of the dead as crowded, it seemed, as the town of the living. Despite this, there was something strangely deserted about the place. The grass between the headstones was long and pale, and when I put a hand on the fence, flakes of rust came off in my hand. I stood there for a while, looking at the graves in discouragement. This had to be the Church of Saint Magda's. But I had no idea where it was in relation to Saint Adela's and the Widow's house. Best to return and ask the Peeing Lady, if she was still there.

She was – but she was not alone. Two men had hold of her, one on each arm, and her yells could be heard several streets away.

'Let go of me, damn you! I done nothing wrong. Let go of me, you bastards!'

One of them pushed her up against the wall, saying something I couldn't catch. The woman stopped struggling.

'Why?' she said in surprise. 'He only asked me where the church was . . .' She looked down the alley, straight at me. The man turned around too, and I could see his face like a small, pale moon in the darkness. He let go of the Peeing Lady's arm and started down the alley towards me.

'Come here,' he said, but I wasn't having any. I turned and ran like a hare with the hounds on her heels.

I wouldn't have thought that I had a lot of running left in me, but it seemed I had. My feet pounded wetly against the cobbles. Through the gate and left, *away* from the church. As far away from the church as possible. I zigzagged through alleys, gates and courtyards, climbed fences and ploughed through middens, pushed on through a narrow pigsty, disturbing two huge and sleepy sows. All the time I picked the narrowest, dirtiest and darkest ways, hoping the men would be too slow, too lazy, too fastidious or simply too big to follow me.

When at last I had to stop, unable to run any further, there were no longer cobbles under my feet, and no longer stone houses with glass-paned windows around me. The street, if it could even be called a street, was a filthy stretch of mud and gravel between walls of rough boards or wattle and daub. Here, there were no such niceties as street signs or water posts or gutters, and certainly no streetlights. The smell of wood fires mixed with a stench of garbage, manure and pee, both animal and human, and in most places the houses were huddled so close that if I put my arms out I could touch a rough and peeling wall on both sides of the alley at once. A horse and cart could never pass here, a handcart only barely. It wasn't hard to figure out that I had ended up in the darkest, dirtiest, and most over-crowded part of Dunark: Swill Town.

I slid to my haunches, leaning my back against a damp and slippery mud wall. Although the hour was so late, there were still voices and other noises to be heard through the thin walls: a rattle of pottery and tin pots, voices raised in quarrel, the thin, shrill scream of a rat hit by a boot or a rock. But no footsteps. I sat there for a small eternity, waiting for someone to appear at the head of the alley. I couldn't make myself believe that I had really and truly escaped them. I wondered what they would do to me when they found me. Would they tie me up again and lead me off, like a hound they no longer had any use for? I was so tired I hardly cared. Or rather, I cared all right, but I was much too worn out to do anything about it. Even if they were to appear at the end of the alley with a dragon on a chain, I would not be able to run another step. And if they did find me now – at least they would no longer be able to use me for a hunting hound. They hadn't caught Nico. And I hadn't led them to the Widow's house.

Exactly how long I squatted there I have no idea. I may even have fallen asleep for a while, open eyes and all. I probably wouldn't have made it to my feet again if I hadn't been so mercilessly cold. Running had made me sweat, but now that I was still, the chill cut me to the bone. My clothes and my hair were soaking wet, and my teeth were rattling incessantly. But still there were no footsteps and no moving shadows at the end of my alley. Maybe I really had escaped. If only I could now find some half-sheltered spot where I could hide out and catch a bit of sleep . . . In the morning, I could then ask directions to the Widow's house, or maybe even find it myself once it was daylight and I could see properly.

My legs trembled under me and would only just support me. The alleys and passages were so boggy that the mud sucked at my feet, and every step was accompanied by a slurping sound. I found a covered stall with three goats in it and had brief dreams of soft, warm straw and maybe even a bit of goat's milk. Nothing came of that — one of them was a mean old billy that started furiously butting his horns against the wattle the minute I made a move to climb it. I was on the verge of just sinking down next to a wall somewhere, when a warm and wonderful scent caught my nostrils. Bread. Newly-baked bread. I followed my nose round a corner and into a small courtyard that seemed a bit less disgusting than the rest of Swill Town. The floor was packed clay, not just filth and mud, and it even looked as if someone swept it once in a while. The walls of the house might be wattle and daub, but they had been whitewashed once in a not too distant past.

One wing of the building had its shutters wide open, and I saw that the whole of the gable end was one huge oven and chimney, built with red bricks. I couldn't see the baker anywhere, but I wasn't foolish enough to sneak into the bakery itself, the way I looked. Even the nicest of bakers would no doubt take a paddle to the backside of such a filthy troll if he found me on his premises. But outside, in the corner by the chimney, stood a cart, close against the wall. If I crawled beneath the cart, I would

162

have shelter from the fine mist of rain which had begun to fall, and the chimney wall would provide heat.

I got down on my belly and wormed my way past the wheel of the cart. It was dark, it was dry, it was warm, there was even a bit of straw to lie on. It was perfect. Or so I thought until I put my hand on something soft and living, and a voice hissed:

'Get off! Get away from me! I got a knife, so you better move!'

EIGHTEEN

Rose

That was how I met Rose. And if I hadn't been so worn out, I might never have said three words to her; probably, I would just have run off. But this was it for me. I had fought against murderers, dragons, full-grown castle guards, and Lady Death herself. At this point, it would take more than a sleepy and frightened girl's voice to scare me off, knife or not.

'There's room enough for two,' I said. 'And if you don't think so, *you* can move, 'cause I'm not walking another step tonight.'

Silence. It was so dark beneath the cart that I could only just make out her face, a paler grey shadow than the rest, with eyes that glittered faintly in the gloom.

'You talk strange,' she said. 'Where're you from?'

'Birches,' I said, before considering that it might not be wise to say too much. Did everyone in town know where the Shamer lived?

'Where's that?' she said. 'Way out in the country?' She made it sound as if 'way out in the country' was the same as 'very slow and very stupid', but I was too tired to argue.

'Yes,' I muttered. 'Way out . . .' The chimney wall was even warmer than I had hoped. I rested against it and let myself be baked. My eyes closed, and my body slowly stopped shaking.

'Why're you so wet?' asked the girl into the darkness.

'It's raining.'

'Not *that* much.' She sounded tense and suspicious. 'Someone after you?'

'No,' I lied. Why couldn't she just shut up and let me sleep?

'There is, too. Why else would you be hiding here?'

'Why are *you* hiding? I just need a place to sleep.'

She was silent for a while. 'If you say so,' she finally said, not sounding very convinced. Yet for some reason, she no longer seemed so suspicious. It was almost as if it made her *calmer* to think that someone might be after me. Strange girl. But I was too tired to wonder, too tired to think, too tired for anything but sleep . . .

Someone's elbow poked me in the side.

'Hey! Hey there, sleepyhead! Wake up!'

I opened my eyes. The light wasn't blindingly brilliant, but it wasn't quite night any more.

'Move. I want out and you're in my way.'

I turned my aching head. A girl with fly-away blonde braids was lying next to me, poking me in the side. Who was that? Where was I? And why was I feeling so sick?

Then it all came back. Mama. The dragon. It was today. It was today, and here I was, lying under someone's cart in a back yard in Swill Town, while Nico and Master Maunus thought I was with the Widow. And the girl with the braids was the one whose hiding place I had shared for part of the night. I closed my eyes again at once, trying not to look her in the face, but she paid no attention.

'Come on, lazybutts. Move!'

'Calm down,' I muttered, not particularly calm myself, and began to sit up.

The moment I moved, the surge of pain from my arm took my breath away. Tears squeezed by my closed eyelids and trickled down my cheeks.

'What's wrong?'

'I've hurt my arm,' I managed to say through clenched teeth. Throb, throb, throb . . . surely it *had* to ease off.

There was a rattle of straw as she moved to look.

'I'll say,' she said. 'You look like a stuck pig.'

I opened my eyes to check. She was right. From well above the elbow and down to the wrist, the sleeve was matted with blood. There would be no sneaking inconspicuously through town like this – anyone who saw that arm would remember me.

I glanced at the girl. She was wearing a striped blouse in an uneven mixture of brown and grey and white, probably knitted from leftover yarn, and underneath the blouse, a long-skirted black dress that was much too big in the waist.

'How much will it cost me to swap clothes with you?' I asked.

'I knew it! There *is* someone after you!'

I pretended not to hear. 'I can pay you four copper

pennies here and now,' I said. 'And more when we get to . . . to a place I'll tell you about if you agree.'

She thought about it.

'And how do I know you won't cheat me? Four pennies – that's cheap for a new dress.'

I didn't know what to say to that. 'I won't cheat you . . .' But I could think of no good, solid arguments to convince her.

'I just got this,' she said, picking at the dress. 'Ma got it from one of the ladies she does laundry for, and it's almost good as new. I'll be in a lot of trouble if . . .' She broke off and tried to catch my eyes, but I wouldn't let her, of course. There wasn't really anything more I could say, so I just sat there, holding my arm and waiting for her to come to a decision.

'Come home with me,' she suddenly said. 'I've got an old skirt you can borrow that's not really fit to wear any more. And the blouse. You can have the blouse now.'

It was my turn to hesitate. Home . . . what was she doing here if she had a home to go to? And if I went with her – what if she had figured out who I was? Or just counted on me being worth something to whoever was 'after me'? But what else was there to do? Besides, she didn't seem like someone who would cheat me. In spite of all her talk about knives and so on.

'Well?' she said. 'You coming, or what?'

I nodded. 'Yes.'

'Then let's go.'

She pulled the long-sleeved blouse over her head and gave it to me. I could see now that I wasn't the only one with a reason to wince this morning. Her neck and shoulder were black and blue all over. She saw me noticing, but she didn't say anything.

'What's your name?' I asked.

'Rose. What's yours?'

Did people here know the Shamer's daughter by name? For a moment I was tempted to call myself by some false name, just to be safe. But something stopped me. Some sense that lying to Rose could cost me a lot, and not just money, either.

'Dina,' I said, watching for a reaction.

She didn't seem surprised to hear a girl's name. Probably, hearing my voice in the dark first, she had never been fooled by the boy's clothes. In any case, she just nodded, spat into her palm and held it out to me, the way people do when they close a deal. I spat too, and we shook on it. I don't think either of us was entirely sure exactly what the deal was. Still, it gave a sense of . . . well, a feeling that we could trust each other.

Rose lived in the narrowest house I had ever seen. You had to go into a gateway between two buildings and up some steps that were hardly more than a ladder, and there, in a room over the gate, lived Rose's family.

'You got to be quiet,' she whispered, climbing the steps. 'Better not wake anyone.'

There was only the one room, a long narrow one. All of one end was taken up by two alcoves, and you could hear someone snoring away behind the bed curtains. There was a cloying smell of spilled beer and unwashed chamber pots. I was happy that this wasn't my home, but surely it was better than a pile of straw under a cart? Rose crouched in front of a chest that had been pushed up against the wall beside one of the alcoves. The lid creaked as she opened it, not very loudly, but enough, it seemed, to wake one of the sleepers.

'Rosie? Is that you?' Someone moved behind one lot of curtains, but the snoring from the other alcove went on.

'Yes, Ma,' whispered Rose. 'Go back to sleep.'

'Where've you been?' Rose's mother appeared, rumpled and bleary-eyed, with grey hair sticking out every which way. She didn't really sound angry or worried, just tired. She looked almost more like a grandmother than a mother, I thought. Certainly she must be much older than Mama. The bare legs poking out from under the nightgown were thin and knobby like a chicken's.

'Around,' Rose said sulkily. If I had spoken to my mother like that, all hell would have broken loose, but Rose's ma just sighed and looked away, almost as if ashamed.

'It's his house, Rosie girl,' she said. 'He's the master now, you know that.'

'So he says.' Rose had lost her whisper and spoke loudly and bitterly.

'Hush, girl . . .' said her mother in a frightened voice. But it was too late. The thunderous snoring stopped, and there was a creaking of bedboards.

'Damn cackling,' snarled a voice from inside the second alcove, and the curtains were ripped aside, so violently that the eye came off the hook and the whole thing ended up on the floor. A young man was glaring at us with extremely bloodshot eyes.

'Who the hell is that?' He pointed at me.

'Friend of mine,' Rose said curtly. 'We'll be leaving. Go back to sleep.'

'Who the hell can sleep through that infernal noise? And what're you doing with your hands in that chest? Whaddya think you're goin' to take?'

'Nothing that isn't mine!'

'Yours? *Yours?* You don't own a crumb or a stitch not of my giving. Hands off that chest and get out of here before I have to teach you a lesson on yours and mine, you thieving little slut!'

'If anyone here's a thief—' Rose shouted, but her mother interfered.

'Don't go yelling at your brother like that, Rosie. Aun, she don't mean nothing by it . . .'

Aun made no answer. He just leaped out of the alcove, shoved Rose's ma to one side, and slammed the lid down so quickly that Rose barely avoided getting her fingers trapped. He put one bare foot on the chest and leaned forward, bringing his face very close to Rose's.

'Where've you been, slut?'

'Nowhere.'

'You know what happens to girls who stay out in the streets at night, don't you? They end up like No Man Kassie. Six pennies a go. Is that how you want to pay me for your room and board?'

Rose stood quite still. She hadn't retreated. She hadn't budged an inch. But she didn't say anything, either. I

170

could see the tension in her jaw, a tiny, tiny trembling.

''Cause if you're not going to pay – you got to learn how to *mind*.' He slowly put his hand on her neck – in exactly the spot where it was already black with bruises. He looked a little bit like a dragon, I thought. He moved like one – slowly, lazily . . . and yet frighteningly dangerous. He was naked except for a pair of blue linen trousers, and his chest and arms were knotted with muscle. He had long, curly chestnut hair, and apart from the bloodshot eyes, he was quite clearly someone Cilla from the mill would giggle over and make calf eyes at. Me, I wouldn't touch him with a poker – unless the poker was a nicely heavy one that could deliver a good, hard blow. How could he do that to Rose? And he was her *brother*!

'I think I gave you an order last night. Remember?'

Rose still didn't speak. Then I saw his grip tighten around her poor bruised neck.

'Remember – slut?'

Still no answer. His knuckles began to whiten with the tightness of his grip. And finally Rose gave a tiny nod.

'What did I tell you to do? Well?'

Rose shot a look at her mother. *Do something*, it said. *Stop him*. But her mother just sat there on the edge of the bed, small and old and freezing, staring at the floor.

'*What did I tell you to do?*' A vicious whisper, accompanied by a jerk that could have snapped a rat's neck.

'You told me to polish your boots,' Rose said in a barely audible voice.

'And did you?'

Silence. Then Rose straightened beneath his grip.

'Polish them yourself.' It was little more than a whisper, but it made Aun stiffen with incredulity.

'What did you say?'

'I said that you can *polish your own damn boots*!' Rose stood there, straight as a candle, yelling the words into his face. He looked like someone who has just swallowed a toad. For a moment nothing else happened. Then he smacked her so hard that he knocked her all the way across the narrow room and into the other wall.

'Don't get smart with me, you little slut!' He seized her and dragged her to her feet only to hit her again.

'Aun . . .' His mother's objection was just a whiny whimper. 'She's your sister!'

'No way she's my sister,' roared Aun, catching hold of one of Rose's fair braids. 'She's a bastard brat you got us whoring around on my father, and I'm kicking her out, right here, right now!'

He dragged her the length of the room and pushed her through the open door, on to the landing outside. 'Get out, whore's brat,' he yelled. 'And take your rag-arsed friend with you!'

It was probably stupid. But I couldn't help myself.

When he turned to me, I caught his eyes.

'*How pitiful.*'

'What the—'

'*Are you really so pitiful? Are you really so scared?*'

Completely stunned, he let go of Rose's braid. But I wasn't done with him.

'You're a real man, aren't you? So big and strong that you dare to hit little girls. Master of the house! Shall I tell you what you are really afraid of? Shall I? You're terrified that we're all laughing at you. And you know what? Maybe we are. *Why not? You're certainly laughable enough!*'

He looked like a clubbed steer. I didn't release him until he bent his head on his own. He was gasping for breath and I think he was about to burst into tears. Without a word, he pushed past Rose and pounded down the steps outside.

Rose and her ma were both staring at me as though I had acquired an extra head.

'How did you do that?' whispered Rose. 'Why didn't he hit you?'

'Seems he's got a sense of shame after all,' I said drily. 'But we'd better not count on a lasting effect. Take what you need from the chest and let's go. I don't have much time.'

Rose came with me, to show me the way and to get her skirt back. And maybe also because she didn't want to be there when Aun returned. She had found a scarf for my hair, and as we walked side by side with one of her mother's baskets swinging between us, we looked like any pair of laundry girls. Except that after a while, I noticed that Rose was sniffling as she walked.

'What's wrong? Does it hurt?' Aun had hit her very hard.

'No.'

'Then what's the—'

173

'Nothing.' Sniff.

I put down my end of the basket, and she had to stop. 'Rose . . .'

'Oh, stop it,' she snarled, tears and temper hoarsening her voice. 'I know what you think of us. Of me. And Ma. But I don't care, see? I don't care!'

'Rose—'

'So what if I'm a bastard? Not my fault, is it? And even bastards have a right to live, don't they?'

'I never said—'

'Oh, it's not what you *said*. You don't have to say a thing. I can tell. You haven't even *looked* at me since . . . since Aun said that about Ma and me.'

So that was it . . . I hadn't looked at her before, either, but it was only now that she had noticed.

'Rose . . . My mother isn't married either.'

'So? Then I don't see what you have to be so high and mighty about!'

'I'm not—'

'Then why won't you look at me?'

I closed my eyes. I *liked* Rose. She was stubborn and she was honest. She wouldn't trick you, the way Cilla had, and she wouldn't turn her back on you, the way Sasia from the inn had done. She was brave enough to stand up to her louse of a brother and tell him to polish his own boots. Somehow, I had allowed myself to have these little daydreams. Everything would turn out just fine, together we would rescue my mother and reveal Drakan's evil deeds to the people of Dunark, and Rose and I would be friends for life . . . and Rose had just popped that particular soap bubble. How could we be friends when we couldn't even look at each other?

After a quick glance up the street, I dragged her and the basket into a narrow, deserted alley. Then, I raised my head and met her eyes.

'My mother has three children and she has never married. Shamers usually don't.'

Rose stared at me. Both cheeks were red and swollen from Aun's blows, and there were tears in her green eyes – tears, and astonishment.

'Shamers . . .' You could practically see the thoughts clicking over in her head. 'You're the Shamer's daughter!'

'Yes. Dina Tonerre.' I waited. Here it was. In a minute, her glance would begin to waver, and she would turn her back on me. She might even call my mother a witch, and me a devil's brat. Enough people had.

She didn't turn away.

She still didn't turn away.

And then pictures started to float between us, as they had between Nico and me back in the cell. Aun hitting her. Aun hitting their mother. Other children from her street, jeering and shouting: 'Whore's brat! Whore's brat!' Oh yes, she was ashamed. Her shame was deep, sincere, and terrible. *But she had no reason to be!*

I don't know exactly how I did it. It was the opposite of making people ashamed of themselves, and yet it was the same thing. I let her see herself. I made her see the brave, stubborn, honest Rose *I* had seen. I showed her that it had never mattered a damn to me that my mother wasn't married. I showed her that it wasn't her fault when Aun hit her, or when he hit their mother. She was

175

stubborn. She fought me. But I succeeded in the end: I took her shame away from her.

Slowly, the alley fell back into place: the cobbles, the walls, the laundry basket between us. I looked at Rose, but in the ordinary way. Tears were still trickling down her cheeks. She didn't say a word. But she took my hand.

Explanations were necessary, of course, and I gave them as quickly as I could. I told her almost all of it. The only thing I left out was the bit about Master Maunus and Nico's hiding place. I didn't dare tell her that – not because I thought she would give us away on purpose, but still. It was a secret that wasn't really mine to give.

Rose wasted no time with words like 'Oh, poor you!' or 'How terrible!' She took a grip on the basket again and said: 'We'd better hurry, then.' She didn't have to say anything else. I simply knew that I was no longer alone.

Dunark was Rose's town, and that made a big difference. Compared with my stumbling, zigzagging run the night before, our way to Saint Adela's and the Widow's house was short, straight and quick, even with me looking over my shoulder half the time to see if anyone was following or showing any unusual interest. I didn't see anyone like that, and so I pushed open the gate to the Widow's herb garden with a sense of relief.

'Come on,' I said to Rose, who was hanging back and looking shy. 'She'll probably give us a good breakfast.'

'Me, too?' Rose asked dubiously. 'But she doesn't even know me . . .'

'You too,' I said. 'That's the way she is.'

I knocked on the blue kitchen door, and almost at once I heard the Widow telling us to enter. And then I was there again, in that blue-painted many-shelved room, half kitchen, half workshop, and homey with the smell of mint and garlic.

'Dina!' said the Widow, looking tense and tired.

'Goodmorrow, Madam Petri,' I said. 'This is my friend Rose . . .' And then I suddenly hesitated, for mixed in with the mint and garlic was a new smell, the sharp, sweet scent of pipe tobacco.

I spun around. And there, behind me, on the bench by the door, sat the Weapons Master from Dunark Castle, blowing bluish smoke rings from his clay pipe.

'About time, girl,' he said. 'We've been waiting for you.'

NINETEEN

The Weapons Master

I would never make it through the door – he was right next to it, and I knew he could move when he wanted to. Was there a back door? This one room was all I knew. I threw a wild look in the Widow's direction. *Help me*, I thought at her, show me the way, scream, *do* something . . . but she just stood there with her arms folded across her chest in a stiff, strange manner, an unreadable expression on her face. Was she the one who had betrayed us, even? I didn't want to believe that, but somebody must have!

'He says he's here to help,' she said.

At first I thought I had misheard. To help? Help whom? Not me, surely?

I looked at him again. He still sat there, puffing on his pipe, nice and easy. He hadn't leaped to his feet, and there was no sign of guards with ropes and sacks.

'There's power in you, Shamer girl,' he said. 'More than you think, perhaps.'

'What do you mean?' I whispered. What was he up to?

178

'I mean that I didn't sleep last night. Because of you, and what you made Her Grace say.'

Her Grace? Did he mean . . . I suppose he meant Drakan's mother. Lady Death. *What we did was justice*, she had said, when I asked her why they had murdered little Bian. That was what the Weapons Master had heard.

'I've served the Raven since I was a lad of sixteen,' he said. 'It wasn't easy for me to believe that young Mesire Nicodemus was a monster who had murdered his own family. Had they not found him so, blood-soaked and clutching the dagger . . . then I don't suppose anyone would have believed it. He still has some explaining to do. But that Drakan wants to kill the Shamer just for saying that Mesire Nicodemus is innocent . . . that must count for something too. Surely her words are not that dangerous – unless they happen to be true? And if the young lord is not the killer, someone else must have done it. Someone else who stood to gain by it.' He wouldn't say it outright, not even here, where he must know that he was not among Drakan's people. If one could be thrown to the dragons for believing Nico innocent – then who knew what could happen to someone who claimed *Drakan* was the murderer?

'Have you spoken to anyone else about this?' asked the Widow.

He blew another smoke ring. 'A few. A few good people I thought I could trust.'

'And?'

'And we will do what we may to save the Shamer and to bring the young lord to safety. Right now, the

Dragon reigns in Dunark. We pray it will not be a long reign, and what may be done to end it, we will do. That, I swear to you.'

'Good,' said the Widow. 'We'll believe you – if you will look Dina in the eyes and repeat that oath.'

He didn't want to – and frankly, I didn't much want to, either. I felt tired and dizzy. My arm hurt, and so did my head. I didn't want to look yet another stranger in the eyes and beyond. Rikert Smith is always saying that we should be careful what we wish for, because wishes sometimes come true. That day – how long ago? It felt like a year – the day I had walked into Birches sulky and lonely, wanting people to look me in the eyes . . . well, I had never once considered that it might be hard on *me* if they did. But the Widow was right; it was the best way to be sure. And if I had learned one thing since that day in Birches, it was that grown-ups were even cleverer than children when it came to tricking, cheating and betraying.

It was a huge effort for him to meet my gaze, but he made himself do it.

'I promise to serve Mesire Nicodemus,' he stated slowly and solemnly. 'I promise to end the reign of the Dragon, if it be in my power. And I promise to help save your mother.'

His glance did not waver.

'Thank you,' I said, believing now that he spoke the truth. Pictures flickered between us, pictures I was too tired to make sense of – a house burning, dust dancing across fallen bodies, a glitter of steel, and a taste of blood. But it was a distant shame, and there were no lies that I could see. 'Only . . . How did the Master find Madam Petri?'

I still held his gaze, and he let me. He even smiled and held out a small piece of paper, yellow and rumpled.

'The note you wanted back so badly. It took a while to figure out the invisible ink, but I managed in the end.'

I took the note. Master Maunus would never have been so incautious as to use names, but there were clues enough if you knew where to look. Not many nieces in Dunark would be able to get hold of such quantities of sleeping draught as Master Maunus asked for. What did he mean to do with it? Drug half the population? Or just one dragon? He and Nico had deliberately not told me their plans.

'Well, Dina?' The Widow was getting impatient. 'Can we trust him?'

'I think so,' I said, releasing the Weapons Master's gaze. He gave a slight shudder and dragged on his pipe, almost as if for comfort.

'Good.' The Widow set four beakers on the blue kitchen table and uncorked a bottle of elderflower wine. 'Then, let's make plans.'

'No,' I said, trying to sound like an adult, or a near-adult, and not like a tired and mulish kid who was about to blubber. 'I won't do it!'

The Widow peered at me, not long enough for it to hurt, just a quick glance to check the expression on my face.

'It's safer,' she said. 'You'll endanger all of us if you

181

insist on coming along. Or do you think they're not searching for you?'

I knew they were. But staying behind, stuck in the Widow's house not knowing what was happening, not knowing if everything was fine or they were all captured or even dead on the cobbles of the Arsenal Court . . . it was like being blindfolded all over again. And I never wanted to be blind again. Not ever.

'It's risky enough as it is,' growled the Weapons Master. Children were supposed to do as they were told, said his voice. And not whine about it, either.

'We'll be back,' said the Widow, gently persuasive. 'We won't forget you or abandon you.'

Great. Now, it seemed, I sounded like a tired and mulish little kid who was scared of being home alone.

'It's not that . . .' Why was the kitchen so cold? I had drawn the sleeves of Rose's blouse over my hands, but my fingers were still chilled and stiff.

'I'll sit with you,' said Rose. 'You won't be alone.'

'Thanks,' I said, meaning it. 'But it's more . . . not knowing what's happening. Not being *there*.'

'You ought to be giving thanks to the Creator that you don't have to be there—' began the Weapons Master, but the Widow cut him off with a small movement of her hand.

'Dina, we *have* to succeed – and we might not, if you're with us. Don't you see that?'

I nodded. Tears were hot in my eyes, and I didn't dare say anything out loud, not wanting to appear both a snotty little kid *and* a cry-baby.

'Would it help if we told you exactly what will

happen? So that you'll know as much as possible?'

I looked at her sideways, careful not to hurt. Maybe she did understand some of how I felt. And deep down, I knew she was right. If someone recognized me – if even one guard happened to see my eyes . . . I cleared my throat. Nodded again.

'All right, I'll stay here.' My voice sounded nearly normal. 'But tell me about it. Tell me *everything* about it!'

The Weapons Master snorted and got to his feet.

'Fine. Excellent. Tell her all. But you'll have to excuse me a while. I've got just a few things to do before we penetrate the castle defences, rescue a couple of heavily guarded prisoners, and make a clean getaway from under the noses of Drakan's three hundred men.'

The Widow put her hand on his arm. 'We couldn't do it without you,' she said quietly. 'I'm glad to know a man who dares to follow his conscience.'

He blushed. He was a square-shouldered, toughened soldier going on fifty, and I don't think anyone had made him blush in years. But the Widow did. He muttered something. Then he hesitantly put his own hand on top of the Widow's and gave it a gentle squeeze.

'Thank you,' he said. 'And, er . . . I really do have to go.'

Once he had left, the Widow patiently and thoroughly went over everything that was to happen. And so I knew it all. I knew that a properly uniformed guard with written orders signed by the Weapons Master himself would soon relieve the Arsenal guard, a little sooner than he was expecting it. I knew that the Weapons Master would that day take it into his head to inspect the walls around the two reservoirs which provided the castle with water. That the Widow would pay a visit to her ageing uncle Maunus. And that the guards in the West Tower would feel very sleepy after having won a bottle of pear brandy from the garrison cook, who just happened to be a very old friend of the Weapons Master. I knew that another guard, walking through the Arsenal Court, would bend to examine the heavy iron ring on the scaffold by the Dragon Gate. I fervently hoped that no one would notice him bringing out a small green bottle and pouring the contents on to the ring, for the bottle contained what alchemists like Master Maunus called Aqua Regia or King's Water – a mixture of hydrochloric and nitric acids, capable of eating through all metals. And I hoped just as fervently that no unexpected visitor would appear while yet another of the Weapons Master's people was busy in the Arsenal, fixing another of Master Maunus's concoctions to the roof beams.

'Is there anything else you would like to know?' asked the Widow, coming to the end of her explanations.

I shook my head.

'Good. I have to leave now. We do not know exactly when Drakan will have your mother led into the Arsenal Court, and everything must be in place before that.'

I nodded. Tears still prickled and stung. As the Widow walked out of that door, my thoughts would follow her. It was a bit like being back in the stone bathhouse, hearing vicious voices paint a picture of what would happen to my mother, without being able to see for myself. Why was it that everything always looked worse in the imagination than in reality?

'I still wish . . .'

'Yes. I know,' said the Widow. 'The waiting is hard. But it *is* better for you to stay here until we come to get you. I don't know how long we will be. You'll just have to be ready to leave at a moment's notice.' She rose, stroked my cheek gently and then suddenly hesitated.

'You're too hot,' she said, feeling my forehead. 'Are you running a fever?'

'No,' I said. I didn't feel hot at all. Chilled, actually.

'Perhaps it's just the tension,' she muttered, more to herself than to me, and tightened her brown shawl around her shoulders. 'Don't let anyone in while I'm gone.'

We waited. The Widow had set out bread and sausage for us, and had told us to open another bottle of elderflower wine. Rose ate and went on eating, as if this loaf was the last bread in the world, but the one bite I took turned to sawdust in my mouth. I just drank, a few sips of wine and beaker after beaker of water from the fancy indoor pump. It was a good thing Rose was there. I think I would have gone crazy, otherwise. It was almost as if I was able to see the Arsenal Court. If I let my eyes rest on one spot too long, on the wall or the table, the pictures would begin to dance the way they did when I looked at another person with my Shamer's eyes. All the time, there were faces, angry eyes and twisted mouths, prodding elbows and trampling feet and fists, clenched and ready to strike. Only when Rose said something did it stop. And it was so much nicer to look at Rose, sitting there in front of me with crumbs on her chin and the sausage grease shiny on her fingers. Her green eyes were alive and curious, not hate-filled like the ones in the pictures.

'What's it like where you live? In that village, what was it called . . .'

'Birches . . .'

'Yes. What's it like? Do many people live there?'

'Some. Not as many as here.' And then I started to tell her about Rikert Smith and his wife Ellyn, about Sasia from the inn and stupid Cilla.

'What a bitch,' said Rose, and in turn told me about their neighbours across the way, whose eldest girl was three times worse than Cilla. It passed the time. The kitchen was gloomy and a bit stuffy with the shutters closed — that way, people knew that the Widow was not home and that the Apothecary was closed to business. A big log was smouldering in the stove, but I still felt chilled and cold.

'I wish I had a brother like yours,' sighed Rose, after I had told her a bit about Melli and Davin. 'Someone who would look after me and someone to talk to, instead of . . .' She broke off, but I knew what she was thinking: someone who called her a whore's brat and hit her and bullied her and threw her out whenever it suited him. Aun was nobody's dream of a brother. More like a nightmare. Davin might be irritating at times, but compared to Aun he was a knight in shining armour.

'I don't get that bit about everything being his,' I said. 'Isn't it your mother's house?'

Rose shook her head, making the blonde braids dance. 'No. It belonged to my stepdad, and when he died, Aun inherited the house and all the furniture and the workshop – my stepdad was a cobbler. But Aun didn't want to fix people's shoes; he sold off the workshop and told us he wanted to be a trader. Like he knew how. He is always shooting his mouth off about all the fine deals he's making, but I think the only real trading he does is bickering with Taddo the Taverner over the price of the next mug of beer!' She sniffed contemptuously. 'And it's so unfair, 'cause if it hadn't been for *my* real da, we never would've been able to stay in the house.'

'You mean, you know who your father is?' I hadn't thought so, not after what Aun said.

'Sure.' Rose nodded. 'I've seen him four times. *My* da was a proper merchant – not a dirty drunk who thinks he's made one hell of a deal if he's managed to buy two sacks of flour for a coppermark. And Aun wasn't so bad back when there was still a bit of money coming, but of course *that* stopped when my da died, 'cause the wife's as tight as they come, though he left her enough, the bitch. She won't even let Ma do the laundry any more. One of the really nice places too, it was, a big stone house in Pewter Street, and the cook used to always sneak me a bite of something when I delivered the clean stuff . . .' She glanced at me. I was picking at a slice of the good wheat bread, crumbling it into tiny pieces, as the thoughts went tumbling one over the other inside my head. Had the Widow reached Maunus and Nico without being stopped? And hadn't it been strange for Rose to sit with the cook in the kitchen, while her father resided in the drawing rooms upstairs, deigning to be seen by his daughter all of four times? Of course, that was more than I could claim. As far as I knew I had never even seen the man who had fathered me.

'What about your da?' asked Rose, as if she could read my mind.

'I don't know who he is. Mama won't say. She says we have a mother and that will have to do. That's the way it's done where the Tonerres come from, or so she says.'

'And where is that?'

'Some of us live in Campana. But originally we came here from a place even further away. A country called Colmonte.'

'Never heard of it.'

'It's *very* far away – out beyond the Circle Sea, Mama says.'

'Wouldn't it be great if—' she began. But I never got to hear the rest of it, for at that moment someone hammered at the door. Not a polite knock, but an angry, scary pounding.

We both sat there, petrified like two leverets in the grass. Rose's eyes were huge with fright. Mine probably were, too. My heart was certainly beating hard enough.

'Open up!' roared an unfamiliar voice, and again someone pounded the door, hard enough to shiver the frame. 'Open up, in the name of the dragon!'

I was on my feet in a second and racing for the back door, and Rose was hard behind me. I jerked and tore at the bolt, but it was too tight and wouldn't budge. Mewling with frustration, I ran back into the kitchen to get a knife or a poker, any sort of tool, but before I had had time to take three steps, there was a crash of splintering wood and daylight flooded the kitchen. A man in armour and dragon tunic pushed the wreckage of the ruined shutters aside and swung across the window sill. Behind him I caught a glimpse of Aun's crimson face.

'There she is!' he screamed. 'The little dark one. That's her — that's the witch's brat!'

TWENTY

Shamer and Shameless

Be careful what you wish for, because wishes sometimes come true. I should never ever have wished to return to the castle, I thought, for now my wish was coming true.

'I *told* her,' Rose whispered, furious and guilt-ridden all at once. 'I *told* her not to tell him where we were.'

I couldn't see her. They had come to catch the witch's daughter, and of course they had brought a sack. I yelled and screamed and fought them as hard as I could, but they were big and fast and ruthless, and they weren't about to let me use my eyes on them. One man yanked at my arm, another swung the sack, and a third whipped the rope around my throat.

'Don't strangle her,' one of them had said. 'Drakan wants her alive and kicking – for now.'

And so they hadn't strangled me – not quite. The sack was scratchy against my face and stank of sheep – probably it had been used for wool. I suppose I was lucky it wasn't a flour sack. It was hard enough to breathe even so. All the time, I felt like I was about to fall because I couldn't see where to put my feet. When

I did stumble, the guard who was holding me jerked me upright again, but as he was holding me by the bitten arm, every jerk brought a dizzying rush of pain, making it still more difficult to stay on my feet.

'I *told* her.'

'Told who?' I mumbled, trying to retain a sense of up and down.

'My ma. But he's always been able to twist her every which way!'

'Your ma? You told your ma about the Widow?' I suddenly remembered them hunched over the chest, heads together, while they were looking for a scarf for my hair. 'You weren't supposed to tell anyone!'

'Yes, but I didn't know . . . It was like – like a precaution. I didn't *know* you then, it was *before* . . .'

Before we had looked into each other's eyes. Back when I was this strange girl who wanted to pay her to borrow her clothes.

'I suppose I—' I began, but received a warning jerk on the arm.

'Shut up and walk, girl,' said the guard holding me.

They were in a hurry, the guards, and they did not want to let us stop or hesitate the least little bit. Around us there were people, a lot of people. I could hear them and feel them, a pushing, shoving crowd that did not want to let us pass.

'Incense! Incense! Buy yer holy incense here!' yelled a hawker practically in my ear. 'Best protection 'gainst the Evil Eye! Get yer incense here!'

'Look!' A woman's voice, shouting. 'They've caught the witch's daughter!'

'Hell and damnation,' muttered the one holding me. 'We'll never get past them now!'

The witch's daughter. The words ran like a hissing echo through the crowd, and the mob tightened around us like a noose.

'Devil brat!' someone screamed.

'She's just a child . . .' said someone else, much closer.

'Make way!' roared one of the guards. 'In the name of the dragon, make way!' There were thuds and blows as Drakan's men had to use shields and spear shafts to force their way through the rout. Something wet and slimy hit my shoulder.

'Rose!'

'I'm here.' Somewhere behind me. 'We're almost at the gates now.'

Suddenly the guard lost his grip on my arm and something tripped me, a foot, perhaps. I fell to my knees and then pitched forward into a kicking, trampling chaos of unseen hands and feet. I tore at the sack, wanting it off, wanting to *see*. Someone grabbed me again and flung me over his shoulder like I was the wool sack. I could feel the cold scales of his mail shirt and thought of dragons.

'Don't wriggle,' he said. 'I might drop you.'

I didn't wriggle. I just kept tearing at the sack. Dangling head down actually made it a little easier, and I managed to drag the cloth partly loose from the cord around my neck. My mouth was now free, making it a lot easier to breathe. But I still couldn't see.

Someone snapped an order to 'Open the gate!' and there was a rattling sound and a squeal of hinges. Space opened up around us, and the noise of the crowd faded. I could hear something else now, the rush and splash of leaping water, and I thought it might be the Raven's Fountain in the Castellan's Court that ordinary people only got to see from afar, through the black iron grille of the Highgate.

'What a circus,' said one of the guards. 'You'd think they'd never seen an execution before.'

'The dragon is new,' said someone else. 'That must be what's pulling such a crowd.'

'Hope they haven't started already,' said a third. 'My partner had found us a great spot at the top of the Garrison Gate, but oh no, Cap'n just had to send me off to fetch the witch's brat.'

'We'll make it,' said the one carrying me. 'I don't think the Dragonlord will let them start without us.'

I had expected the noise to start up again as we approached the Arsenal Court. But although I could feel the presence of the hundreds, or even thousands of people packed into the walled space of the court, they were strangely quiet.

Then I heard my mother's voice.

'**Look inside,**' she said, and although it must have taken a terrible effort to reach that many people, she sounded unstrained and quite close, as if she were standing right next to me. '**Look at yourselves. Is this right? Is this a good and worthy act? I have done only my right and proper duty. Has the truth become such a stranger here that it must cost me my life?**'

The guards came to a complete halt. I was suddenly on my own two feet again, and no one was holding me.

I tore off the sack. Finally, I could see.

All of the huge Arsenal Court was packed with people. I think there were more than even Drakan had counted on. Spectators were sitting on the roofs of the lowest buildings – the smithy, the bathhouse and the Garrison Gatehouse – and the windows of the East Wing were likewise crowded. Some had brought carts to stand on, to raise themselves above the mob for a better view. Only the area immediately around the scaffold and the chained dragon was clear. Although everyone wanted to see it, nobody wanted to get *too* close.

Right now, though, no one was looking at the dragon. Some were standing there with bent heads, looking at the ground. The rest were staring at my mother.

They had chained her hands and blindfolded her, but they had not known that a Shamer may command just with her voice alone, if she is strong enough. She stood there on the scaffold, small and slender between two towering guards, all alone among hundreds of people who had come to see her die. She was not dressed in shiny silk and brocade like Dama Lizea and the other grand ladies on the palace balcony. She wore the same brown dress she had left home in five days ago, and her chestnut hair had lost its sleek shine and fell in uncombed tangles to her waist. But not one of the grand ladies, not one of Drakan's armoured men of war, nor Drakan himself . . . not a one of them could have done what she was doing.

She couldn't see them, but she made them see themselves. That's why it was so quiet. That's why hundreds of people bowed their heads and were silent.

It was a moment when anything could happen. And Drakan must surely know how dangerous it was. He had put himself on a gold chair on the balcony, raised high above the crowd. He had probably set it up that way in order to look more like a lord. Now he leaped to his feet and shouted into the silence.

'Oh yes, she's very good, the witch! But a Shamer she is not!'

My jaw dropped. How could he say that; how could he stand there and say that when every single man and woman in the court could feel *exactly* how strong a Shamer my mother was? But while every other person there was standing motionless, forced into seeing themselves with a Shamer's eyes, Drakan swung himself adroitly over the balcony rail and dropped into the courtyard below. They had built a ramp to the scaffold for the dragon to climb, once they gave it enough chain to do so. But Drakan beat the dragon to it, at least for a while. He ran up the ramp in a few long strides and reached my mother so quickly that it almost seemed like magic.

'What you feel isn't shame, good citizens. It's witchcraft! Why should you feel ashamed? This is no Shamer but a witch in the pay of the murderous monster, Nicodemus. And you have come to see her receive just punishment! *If she were a true Shamer, could I do this?*' And he ripped the blindfold off, seized my mother by the chin, and stared into her eyes.

A gasping rush went through the Arsenal Court. Even I, who had seen him do it before, suffered a moment's doubt. Could he really have done what I thought he had done? It seemed inconceivable that a man could kill three people and afterwards stand there and face my mother without blinking.

Mama was silent herself for a long moment. Perhaps she too felt the shock. Then she spoke again, quietly, but loudly enough for everyone there to hear.

'I have never before met a completely shameless human being. It must be strange to have no conscience at all.'

But people didn't understand. All they could see was that he met her eyes without fear. That the flaw was in him and never in her Shamer's gift – that, they could not comprehend. And if a few of them did understand, they pushed the inconvenient knowledge aside. They would rather believe in Drakan than in the ugly mirror image she had shown them moments before. I could see them straightening, shaking off that nagging sense of shame.

Drakan noticed too. He let go of my mother and turned to the crowd. 'You have lost a lord,' he shouted. 'I have lost a father. My beautiful sister-in-law, her unborn child, my little nephew Bian . . . Am I to look on meekly while their murderer walks away unpunished? This woman had her part in their deaths. Does not she deserve to die?'

A muttering spread through the crowd.

'If she's a witch . . .'

'The boy was only four . . .'

'He looked her in the eye. No one can look a true Shamer in the eye . . .'

'. . . in the Monster's pay . . .'

'Let the witch die!'

'Let the witch die!'

'Let the witch die!'

I couldn't stand it any more.

'Drakan did it!' I yelled, pushing through the crowd to reach my mother. '*Drakan* killed them!'

No one seemed to hear me. But both Drakan and my mother saw me. My mother opened her mouth to say something, but Drakan caught hold of her chained hands and pulled her close and himself said something that made her keep silent. She no longer looked calm; there was a look on her face of utter despair, and I forgot everything, forgot to think, forgot all except the one thing: I wanted to be with my mother.

I would never have reached her alone. But Drakan gestured for two of the guards by the scaffold to open the way for me.

'It was Drakan,' I told my mother. 'Drakan did it . . .'

I probably thought my mother would make them listen. I had imagined that she would say '***Drakan did it***' in such a way that everyone would believe it. She didn't. She looked at me with those desperate eyes and said, very firm and low:

'Be *quiet*, Dina!'

Drakan reached out and seized me by the scruff of the neck. I had forgotten how quickly he could move.

'Well, Medama Tonerre,' he said, without raising his voice. 'May we *now* have the truth about Mesire Nicodemus? Or shall the witch's daughter share the witch's fate?'

'Oh, *Dina* . . .' There were tears in my mother's eyes. 'Why didn't you just run?'

Drakan jerked his head at one of the scaffold guards. 'Bring me another set of irons.'

One of them threw a length of chain on to the scaffold and he quickly bent to twist it around my ankle and fasten it to the same ring to which they had chained my mother.

'Well, Medama?' His voice was cold as ice. 'Is he not guilty?'

My mother was deathly pale. She stared at him, and he met her eyes as if she was not who she was.

'You are no kind of man,' she said at last. 'You have no more conscience than a beast.'

He didn't like that. For a moment his shoulders tensed as if he was going to hit her, and my own hands tightened into fists in defence. Then he gave a brief nod, not in agreement, but because he had reached a decision.

'As you wish, Medama. Perhaps you will change your mind after a closer look at a *real* beast.' He raised his voice. 'Pay out the dragon's chain!' There was a rattle and a grinding of gears from the Dragon Gate. 'Or perhaps Medama believes that her murderous friend will come and rescue her at the last moment? I hope he'll try – I most certainly hope he will try!'

He turned and sauntered down the ramp, unhurried despite the dragon's advance. Perhaps he had no reason to be scared of them, I thought angrily. Any dragon fool enough to take a bite out of him would no doubt drop dead then and there! The guards surrounding my mother were decidedly more nervous and leaped off the scaffold with inelegant haste.

The dragon moved forward slowly. Sunlight glistened on the grey scales with each step, and the long, thick tail swung lazily from side to side. At the foot of the ramp the dragon paused, tasting the air with its forked tongue. How much chain had they given it? Enough to reach us?

Mama brought her chained hands up and drew me close. She couldn't hold me, but she lowered her cheek on to my hair.

'Get behind me,' she whispered. 'He won't let it eat a child. People wouldn't let him.'

After all those cries of 'devil brat' and 'witch spawn' I wondered whether there was anything at all that the people of Dunark wouldn't let Drakan do. But that wasn't the reason why I shook my head.

'No,' I said, so softly that only she could hear. 'Let's stand quite still. I don't think dragons have very good eyesight. And maybe . . . maybe something is about to happen.'

But if something was to happen, it had better be soon. The dragon put one foot on the ramp, testing it; then it scuttled forward another few steps. It might not be able to see us very well – but it had our scent now. It opened its jaws, and the rank stench of spoilt meat washed over us. I looked straight into the bluish-purple maw, close enough for me to count all the needle-sharp fangs, and the sight made my arm burn and throb even more. I made a noise, not a scream, just an involuntary little squeak. My mother raised her head.

'Drakan,' she called in a harsh and desperate voice. 'Wait . . .'

At that moment a booming explosion rattled the fancy glass panes of the palace, and fat black columns of smoke billowed from the narrow window slits of the Arsenal. The dragon closed its mouth and blinked – it looked weird, the eyelid coming up from below. Someone in the crowd was shouting, telling people to get away, run for their lives, the Arsenal was on fire and any minute we would all be blown into the next world.

'It's going to blow! Run!' The shouting spread.

People were screaming and pushing and falling over each other. Those who could began to run. Suddenly there were only two guards anywhere near the scaffold. One of them, a brave man, turned and raced *towards* the Arsenal, presumably to try and put out the fire before it reached all the black powder stored in there and blew the whole castle sky high. The other leaped on to the scaffold, drew a hammer from his belt and landed a mighty blow on the ring to which my mother and I were chained. Weakened by Master Maunus's Aqua Regia, the iron ring sprang apart at the second blow. The guard straightened, and I could see that the face beneath the helmet's noseguard was Nico's.

'Run,' he said, grabbing my mother's elbow and spinning her around. 'Run for the Dragon Gate.'

'But . . . the dragon!'

'My meat,' he said. He drew a bottle from beneath his tunic, pulled out the cork and turned to the monster. 'Draco Draco . . .' he called, like he had that night in the Pit. He flung the hammer straight at its face. The dragon hissed and opened its cavernous jaws – which proved to be a mistake on the dragon's part. With a deft, precise flip, Nico tossed the bottle straight into its mouth. The dragon immediately lost interest in everything else. Hissing and spitting, it clawed at its own face with long black talons.

'*Run*, I said,' yelled Nico. 'The Dragon Gate!'

Mama and I took off, rattling like a tinker's cart what with the chains and all. Only, I didn't make it to the ramp. A sharp jerk of the chain whipped my feet from under me, and I fell to the scaffold in a dizzy, breathless heap.

'You stay here,' Drakan said, planting his foot on my back while I was still waiting for the world to stop spinning. 'And then we'll see how far your mother wants to run. Or perhaps your brave knight there is going to act the hero and try to save you? What say you, Nico? Shall we play?' He drew his sword, and there was a superior kind of ease about the way he handled it. I remembered one of Nico's memories: the day he had flung his sword into the canal and been beaten by his father for it to within an inch of his life. Was it still there, I wondered, rusting in the weedy green water, or had someone fished it out? Nico certainly hadn't touched it, nor any other sword, no matter how hard or how often his father beat him. Yet now he drew the one he had borrowed along with the uniform.

'Let her go,' he said.

'Come and get her.' Drakan smiled, swishing his bright blade through the air in a lightning 'S'.

Nico advanced up the ramp, not at a normal walk but

in a series of flat leaps, always right foot forward. You could tell he had actually been taught how to fence, once. But Drakan parried his first lunge with ease, nearly twisting the sword from Nico's grasp.

'Try again,' he sneered. He hadn't even had to remove his foot from my back. 'You *must* be able to do a *little* better than that.'

I managed to twist my head to one side for a better look at Nico. He looked pale and scared, yet at the same time strangely calm. Then I could see nothing but legs for a few seconds, as Nico launched a second attack. The blades clashed with a bell-like sound, and this time Drakan had to move his foot. I rolled to one side and caught a bright glimpse of flying metal, and when I looked at Nico again, I saw that he had lost the sword and was standing there, unarmed before Drakan's blade.

'Too bad, little Nico,' said Drakan. 'You should have taken a few more lessons, you know.' He raised his own sword for the final blow. I wrapped myself around his leg, trying to trip him up, but it wasn't my efforts that caused him to yelp and grab his calf. To the rest of us, it seemed almost as if he had been stung by some giant wasp. Nico was quick to take advantage. He caught his own sword again, swung it like a hammer and hit Drakan on the head with the flat side of the blade. Drakan keeled over backwards and fell without a sound.

'What happened?' Nico said, looking confused. 'Did you bite him?'

'No,' I said. I hadn't even thought of that. And then I caught sight of Rose, who had come out of her hiding place *below* the ramp.

'I told you I had a knife,' she said. And she really did, clutched in her right hand, a small, rusty one whose blade was now red with Drakan's blood.

'Who are you?' Nico was looking at her like she was some kind of ogre, sprung from the bowels of the earth.

'This is my friend Rose,' I said proudly. And *then* we all ran for the Dragon Gate.

Somebody, Nico I think, boosted me over the gate and into the Pit. Master Maunus was there, and the Weapons Master, and three of his men. We hurried across the damp ruins to the reservoir wall, past at least one dragon coiled around a broken pillar in the midday sun. It hissed at us, but made no move to attack. We were too many, and armed with spears that they had learned to respect. Getting up the crumbling reservoir wall was a nightmare. There were cracks aplenty, and Nico helped me when my stupid arm wouldn't work, but the water oozing through the cracks made hand- and footholds slippery, and even the fingers of my good hand ached with the chill. And all the time we were in a tearing, desperate hurry, because Drakan's men would not stay stunned and confused for ever, and we couldn't count on the dragons to stop them any more than they had stopped us. As we were running along the top of the reservoir wall as quickly as we dared, we heard shouts below and saw a couple of guards move cautiously into the Pit, spears at the ready. The Weapons Master was crouched on top of the wall still, working furiously with flint and steel. Then he too came tearing along, faster than any of us, yelling for us to jump on to the roof of the bathhouse

NOW. I hesitated a bit – the drop looked steep to me, and I felt enormously dizzy as it was, but Nico grabbed me round the waist and leaped, carrying me with him. We hit the roof with a thump that went all the way up my backbone and into my skull.

'Nico, you idiot—' I snarled at him and would have said more, but at that moment there was a BOOM, and the roof shook so beneath me that I fell to my knees. Bricks and other debris came crashing down on us and Nico wanted me to lie all the way down and protect my head, but I was staring in fascination as the whole reservoir wall cracked open from top to bottom and a huge wave of water and shattered rock shot out from the crack and started sweeping down into the Pit below.

'Holy Saint Magda,' muttered one of the Weapons Master's men appreciatively. 'That was a good one, Master!'

The Weapons Master looked down at dragons and men struggling in the churning waters below and didn't look nearly as pleased with his handiwork.

'Better than letting all that powder blow up in the Arsenal itself,' he growled. 'And let's not waste the time it's bought us.'

From the bathhouse roof we climbed into the Palace Gardens behind the North Wing. My ears still rang, and the sharp smell of cordite tore at the lining of my nose. A lot of the glass panes in the Orangery had shattered with the blast, and we had to move carefully among the peach and lemon trees, accompanied by a constant tinkling of broken glass. I remember that sound and the way it blended in with the ringing in my ears. I remember staring at a particularly big lemon and thinking how good that would taste, tart and fresh in my dried out, ashy mouth. After that, things got a bit fuzzy for a while. I know that the garrison cook, the Weapons Master's good friend, lowered a rope ladder down to us from the West Tower, but I don't remember climbing it. The way Nico tells it, the Weapons Master himself had to sling me across his shoulder 'like a sack of potatoes', as he charmingly puts it.

Then there were only my mother's eyes, eyes that couldn't be refused.

'Wake up, Dina. I know you aren't feeling well. But you *have* to walk now. We'll never get through the streets if we have to carry you. Do you hear me? Come on. On your feet. One foot in front of the other. *Walk!*'

I walked. What else was there to do? All the way across Dunark to Swill Town, where Rose knew of a breach in the city walls and a path, the Cockle Way, that the Swill Towners used to get down to the mud flats below Dun Rock.

'We dig for mussels at low tide,' she said. 'To sell and to eat.'

Nico muttered that mussels probably wasn't all that was smuggled into Dunark by that path, but I didn't see what he had to complain about. He was glad enough that the breach and the path existed then, wasn't he?

The path was hard and careful going at a time when I could barely stand. But finally we reached the flats below. The air was briny and damp, and above us sea gulls circled, crying out in shrill voices. There were ten of us now: two guards that the Weapons Master thought he could trust, the Weapons Master himself, the garrison cook, the Widow, Master Maunus, Nico, Mama, Rose and me.

'What do we do now?' asked Mama, looking down at her hands so as not to make the others anxious with her eyes.

'We hide among the reeds by the river. This evening, a barge will come.'

'With a skipper we can trust?'

'My brother-in-law,' said the cook curtly.

'How much further do we have to walk?'

'A bit further,' answered the cook. 'No more than an hour.'

And so we walked a bit further.

The cook seemed to be in charge now, which made sense as he obviously knew the flats well and was fresher and more alert than any of us. Sometimes we were told to get down on our bellies. Then we would lie for a while in the soft black mud, looking at the yellow-green reeds in front of our faces, until he told us to get up again. Lying like that was almost pleasant – better than walking, anyway. If only I hadn't been so terribly thirsty. I would have drunk from the dark, brackish water in the canals if my mother hadn't stopped me, saying that if I did that, I would most certainly get even sicker.

'Are you all right?' asked Rose, frowning worriedly.

'Fine,' I lied. What was the point of saying anything else? There was nothing to be done right now. Mama was watching me very carefully, but not even she suggested a rest. It was simply too dangerous.

At long last we reached the hiding place the cook had decided on. The reeds here were tall and thick, a virtual forest for us to hide in. The Weapons Master used his sword to harvest some rushes to make a sort of bed for us. It made for a scratchy mattress, but at least it was drier than the mud. I was shaking with cold now, even though the sun was still high in the sky and little black flies were buzzing in the afternoon heat.

'Right,' said my mother. 'Let me see that arm now.'

I didn't want to. I didn't want to have it poked and prodded and stirred up any more. It was throbbing all the time now. But when Mama used that tone, I knew better than to argue. Carefully she eased Rose's striped blouse over my head, but the arm had soaked through its makeshift bandage again, and the sleeve was sticky with dried blood and stuff. I clenched my jaw until my teeth hurt, but by the time my mother got that sleeve off, the tears were flowing anyway. The bandage was even worse – one caked up, stiffened, bloody mess. When she finally got that off, I was crying so hard I could barely see. Mama looked speechlessly at the triangular wounds for much too long. There were angry red streaks now, and yellow matter in two of the wounds.

'Is there any way at all to get clean water?' she asked.

'Not until the barge gets here,' said the Weapons Master. 'The river water is anything but clean, and we dare not risk a fire. The smoke would be visible for miles.'

Mama asked no more questions. She tore the bottom off her undershirt to make a fresh, if not quite clean, bandage for my arm. The blouse was disgusting, but there was nothing else to wear, and I was freezing like a little dog.

'I thought that arm was doing better,' said Nico in an embarrassed tone.

'It was,' I muttered sulkily. 'Until everybody and his brother John started jerking it around.'

'Sleep if you can,' said Mama and held my hand like the time I was seven years old and horribly ill with the whooping cough. And I slept.

When I woke up, the evening star hung just above the reeds, and the sky was dark blue and soft like velvet to look on. Mama was no longer there, but Nico sat on one side of me and Rose on the other.

'Is the barge here yet?' I asked.

'No, but they think they can see it now,' answered Nico. Rose sat in a slump, looking half asleep.

We were silent for a while. I glanced at Nico, who was staring at the evening star as if expecting it to tell him something.

'Nico?'

'Mmm?'

'That time . . . in the Arsenal Court. When you hit Drakan . . .'

'Yes,' he said drily. 'I haven't exactly forgotten.'

'You hit him with the flat side of the blade.'

'Yes.'

'You could have used the edge. You could have killed him.'

He made no reply.

'Nico – after everything he's done . . . Why didn't you? Why didn't you kill him?'

He took a deep breath and snatched a quick look at me.

'I don't really know,' he muttered. 'I thought I'd killed him once already. I just couldn't do it again, somehow.'

We sat there silently, looking at the evening star together. My arm hurt like hell, but I felt less woozy for having slept a little. Then there was a rustling in the reeds, and the Widow and my mother appeared.

'The barge is here,' said the Widow. 'We have to go now.'

Nico helped me to my feet. My legs were wobbly and uncertain, and it was a while before I noticed that Rose had made no effort to follow us.

'Come on,' I said.

She shook her head. 'No. It's best to say goodbye now.'

'What do you mean? Where are you going?'

'Home.'

'Home?'

'To Swill Town. To Ma.' She couldn't quite bring herself to mention Aun, I noticed.

'Are you crazy?' I said angrily. 'Do you think you can just waltz back home as if nothing has happened? You stuck a knife in Drakan's leg, Rose!'

She looked up at me, and her eyes were bright with tears. But she didn't cry, wouldn't *let* herself cry.

'And where else do you suppose I can go?' Her voice was harsh and hostile, but I knew that was not how she felt inside.

'With us, of course. Right, Mama?'

Mama nodded. 'Rose would be very welcome. We can write a letter to your mother to reassure her. But Dina is right. You can't return to Dunark.'

Rose's lips trembled.

'You mean that?'

'Of course!'

'But . . .'

'But what?'

She sat there, tearing a reed into tiny pieces with sharp little jerks.

'It's just that . . . there isn't anyone . . . I mean, I don't know anyone . . .' She got stuck and started over again in the belligerent tone I was beginning to know quite well. 'It's easy for you to be brave. You've got your mother and your family and Nico and . . . and I don't have anyone. And . . . I've never been outside Dunark before.'

'You've got me,' I said, slightly hurt.

'And me,' said Nico. 'I happen to owe you quite a lot. You may have forgotten that, but I haven't.'

Rose was still picking the reed apart, into ever tinier pieces. I wanted to grab hold of those jabbing, picking hands and make them stop, but I didn't dare. One had to be careful with Rose. She was strong, but also vulnerable. And no one was allowed to feel sorry for her. She wouldn't let them.

Finally the hands were still and the last fragments of the reed fluttered down, coming to rest in the mud beside her.

'Look at me.'

It came so quietly, and I was so surprised by it that I thought I hadn't heard her right.

'What did you say?'

Rose got to her feet. 'Look at me,' she said, a bit more loudly. 'Look at me. Until I know that I dare.'

Sometimes there are things that simply can't be put into words. Things inside you, I mean. That's how I felt right then. I didn't say anything because I couldn't. But I looked my friend straight in the eye until she could feel that I *knew* she was a strong and brave girl who dared do practically anything.

TWENTY-ONE

Home

It would have been a good place to end – there among the reeds with Rose and me, and Nico, and Mama, and the evening star. But that's not how it goes. Not in real life. In real life, the story always goes on. And that's why I have to tell the next bit, even though I don't want to.

It was two weeks before we made it back to Birches. The trip could be made in little more than half a day on fresh horses, but we didn't have fresh horses, or even fresh legs. I became ill with wound fever and couldn't stay on my feet at all. The cook's brother-in-law brought us to this tiny hamlet, just the four houses, in the middle of the Dun Marsh, west of Dunark, where Birches lay east. We hid out there, until I began to get better. And the journey was not a swift ride along the road, but a weary slog along paths and dykes and overgrown trails almost invisible to the human eye.

Finally we could see the hill and the tall, pale birches that had given the village its name. And oh, how I yearned to go to sleep in my own bed up in Cherry

Tree Cottage, waking with Davin and Melli to pad into the kitchen for a breakfast of porridge and Mama's blackcurrant tea.

This was one wish that would never come true. Cherry Tree Cottage didn't exist any more. As we rounded the last curve of the road there were no whitewashed buildings waiting to greet us. There was just a ruin of broken bricks and blackened beams, jutting at the sky like the spikes on a frightened animal. Everything had been destroyed. Even the orchard had been burned down. The cover for the well was smashed, and in the well itself bobbed the bloated remains of our little piebald goat. It would be years before anyone could drink from that well again. They had butchered all the animals they had been able to catch and left most of them just lying there. There were dead chickens and rabbits all over the place. A single surviving hen was picking its way through the rubble when it caught sight of us. It squawked and fled, beating its stubby wings frantically.

At first we all stood there like a bunch of statues. Then Mama gave a strangled kind of shriek and started running towards the village. I knew exactly what she was thinking. None of us was in any doubt that this was Drakan's vengeance. And Mama was terrified that that vengeance might also have struck at Davin and Melli.

'I wish I'd killed him,' said Nico between clenched teeth. 'This wouldn't have happened.'

'There's no way to know that,' I said distantly, my mind in another place altogether. Davin and Melli. 'There's his mother, too.' But oh, how I wished he had

213

used the edge and not the flat of that sword. If anything had happened to Davin and Melli . . . My feet unstuck themselves and I stumbled after my mother, still not able to really run.

Mama met me before I'd reached even the outskirts of the village.

'They're all right,' she shouted. 'They're all right!'

It turned out that they had still been with Rikert and Ellyn when Drakan's men arrived, and they had had time to hide in the loft above the smithy before the wreckers reached the village. Drakan, who remembered that I had a brother, had tried to win over the villagers with fancy words and promises of pay, but when it really mattered, Birches looked after the Shamer's children after all. Even Beastie was unharmed, though Davin had had to hold his nose all afternoon to keep him from barking at Drakan.

That night, we sat in Ellyn's kitchen and tried to get used to the idea that there was no going 'home to Cherry Tree Cottage' any more. It was strange. One villager after the other came by with gifts and food and things they 'really had no use for'. They behaved almost as if it was their fault that Cherry Tree Cottage was a blackened ruin. And it wasn't their fault. On the contrary – they had helped save what was most important, after all. I had never actually felt as warmly towards the miller and his family as I did that night. All of which did not change the simple fact that we could not stay in Birches.

Now we were all of us homeless. The Widow could not return to her house and garden behind Saint Adela's, and Rose could not go back to her ma and the narrow room above the gate in Swill Town. Master Maunus probably missed his workshop the most, with its powders and jars and alembics. And Nico – in a way, Nico had lost a whole town.

'We could go to Grandmother,' said the Widow tentatively. 'In the Highlands.'

'I suppose we could,' said Master Maunus, looking less than thrilled at the thought. 'I suppose we could. But if I had *wanted* to spend my life looking at sheep and drinking malt spirits, I wouldn't have gone to Dunark in the first place.'

'She would make us welcome. And even Drakan will think twice before taking on an entire Skayland clan. We would be safe.'

'Safe,' sighed Mama. 'That sounds very tempting right now.'

Master Maunus is fond of claiming that there are more sheep than people up here. That may well be – but there *are* still people. They talk differently from us lowlanders, but not so much so that I can't understand them. We have just raised the roof on our new cottage and covered it with turf – that's the way they do it here. Almost the entire Kensie clan helped us do it.

Afterwards, there was a party, and Rose and me learned all the steps to the Bear and the Salmon, which is a wild and fast and whirly Skayland dance during which the girls are thrown from one man's arm to the next, spinning like tops. It was fun, but afterwards my arm ached irritatingly. It's still not back to normal and may never be, and I thought my usual black thoughts about Cilla.

Tonight we get to sleep in the cottage for the first time. There is a heady, wonderful smell of new wood all around me. I still miss Cherry Tree Cottage – I probably always will – but I think I could be happy here. In any case, I have Mama and Davin and Melli to share it with. Mama and Davin and Melli – and Rose.

Afterword

Professor Kimberley Reynolds, University of Newcastle

Every now and then a writer appears who seems to speak to and for a particular moment – in her gripping series of Shamer books, Lene Kaaberbol proves herself to be such a writer. This is first-class storytelling. In these days of political spin, the idea that there could be someone who cuts to the truth and makes it visible to all is deeply attractive; but Kaaberbol's Shamers are more than human lie detectors. A Shamer is a public figure with an inherited power to compel those who meet her eyes not only to confess to wrongdoing, but also to see their actions clearly. To look into a Shamer's eyes is like putting the self under a microscope that filters out and magnifies every petty, mean and vicious action in a person's life. No one enjoys it, but admitting to misdeeds can be a relief, and the certainty it brings to the powers that administer justice is enviable.

Since reading the Shamer books, I have frequently wished a Shamer could be produced to make presidents and prime ministers, dictators and abusive soldiers look to their actions. If we were unable to fool ourselves and others with partial truths, the world would undoubtedly be a fairer and more equable place.

But a Shamer isn't a machine, and as always, power comes at a cost. This series of four books traces the life and trials of Dina Tonerre, who has inherited her mother's ability to shame. Shamers are not popular; few willingly look into their eyes, and even fewer like what they see there. Shamers are social outcasts, and for eleven-year-old Dina, this makes her gift seem like a curse. In the course of the series, however, she learns to understand and value the power she has inherited, and to appreciate the small band of family and friends who support her, including her older brother Davin, who feels responsible for his mother and sisters, and guilty that they have had to deal with enemies while he is left at home.

The Shamer books are fantasies, and they are set in a familiar landscape that contains dragons, swords and castles, and in which the battles between good and evil are not played out on television or computer screens. Although clearly not a realistic reflection of the world we know, like all the best fantasies, the books speak forcefully about this world. Not only is the truth manipulated and corrupted by charismatic leaders, but the distinctions between good and evil are also difficult to distinguish.

By following the events that afflict the Tonerre family, readers are reminded that it *is* important to stand up for what you believe, and that even one person can make a difference in the course of events. The series provides a dose of energy and optimism to counter the apathy-inducing effects of modern life.

The Shamer books also reflect the concerns of modern life in many other ways. Dina's mother is a single parent and a working mother at that. Although she has provided a valuable service to her community for years, when a powerful enemy spreads rumours that she is a witch, the fact that she is a woman with knowledge and power becomes a source of danger to her, as has been true for many women throughout history. In the same way, when Dina's father, who has played no part in raising her (she does not even know who he is) decides he wants what her gift can give him, she is caught between warring parents and forced to make unsatisfactory compromises.

Just as disturbingly and topically, the devastating effects of war and persecution make refugees of the Tonerre family, and they soon find out how difficult it is to maintain life and a sense of identity when you have no home and those in power spread false information and create biased legislation to control or even eradicate you. Perhaps more relevant than all of these issues are the ethical questions the books raise about relationships, power, trust, abuse – and what it means to be a hero. Dina's friend Nico, heir to the throne, has a principled dislike of swords and battles, but he and readers have to decide whether it is sometimes right to fight – and kill – in a good cause.

Though never preaching, the four Shamer books hold up a mirror to us all and ask that we think through the consequences of action and inaction. The books make gripping reads and, when finished, they linger in the mind. This is the stuff of classic fiction.